THE ASTROSMURF ★★

Peyo

THE ASTRO SMURF

That's one small step for a smurf...
...one giant leap for Smurfkind! This is the best smurf of my life!
You know, I wonder if this planet is inhabited?
KAYAAA! KAYAAA!
IT IS!

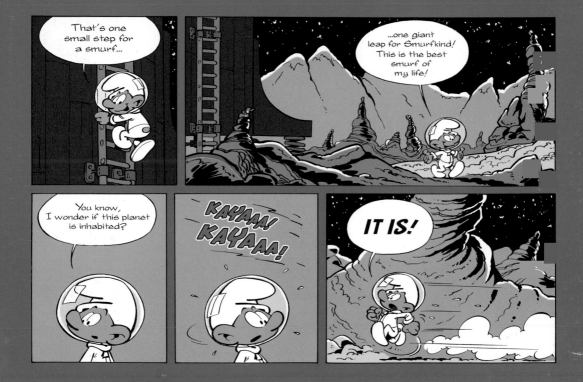

A SMURFS GRAPHIC NOVEL BY PEYO

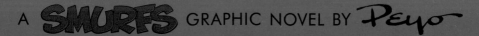

PAPERCUTZ™
NEW YORK

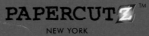

SMURFS GRAPHIC NOVELS AVAILABLE FROM PAPERCUTZ ™

1. THE PURPLE SMURFS
2. THE SMURFS AND THE MAGIC FLUTE
3. THE SMURF KING
4. THE SMURFETTE
5. THE SMURFS AND THE EGG
6. THE SMURFS AND THE HOWLIBIRD
7. THE ASTROSMURF

COMING SOON:

8. THE SMURF APPRENTICE
9. GARGAMEL AND THE SMURFS

The Smurfs graphic novels are available in paperback for $5.99 each and in hardcover for $10.99 each at booksellers everywhere.

Or order through us. Please add $4.00 for postage and handling for the first book, add $1.00 for each additional book. Please make check payable to NBM Publishing. Send to: PAPERCUTZ, 40 Exchange Place Suite 1308, New York, NY 10005 (1-800-886-1223).

THE ASTROSMURF ★★

SMURF™ © Peyo - 2011 - Licensed through Lafig Belgium -

English translation Copyright © 2011 by Papercutz.
All rights reserved.

"The Astrosmurf"
  BY PEYO

"The Smurf Submarine"
  BY PEYO

Joe Johnson, SMURFLATIONS
Adam Grano, SMURFIC DESIGN
Janice Chiang, LETTERING SMURFETTE
Matt. Murray, SMURF CONSULTANT
Michael Petranek, ASSOCIATE SMURF
Jim Salicrup, SMURF-IN-CHIEF

PAPERBACK EDITION ISBN: 978-1-59707-250-2
HARDCOVER EDITION ISBN: 978-1-59707-251-9

PRINTED IN CHINA APRIL 2011 BY WKT CO. LTD.
3/F PHASE I LEADER INDUSTRIAL CENTRE
188 TEXACO ROAD, TSEUN WAN, N.T., HONG KONG

DISTRIBUTED BY MACMILLAN
FIRST PAPERCUTZ PRINTING

THE ASTROSMURF

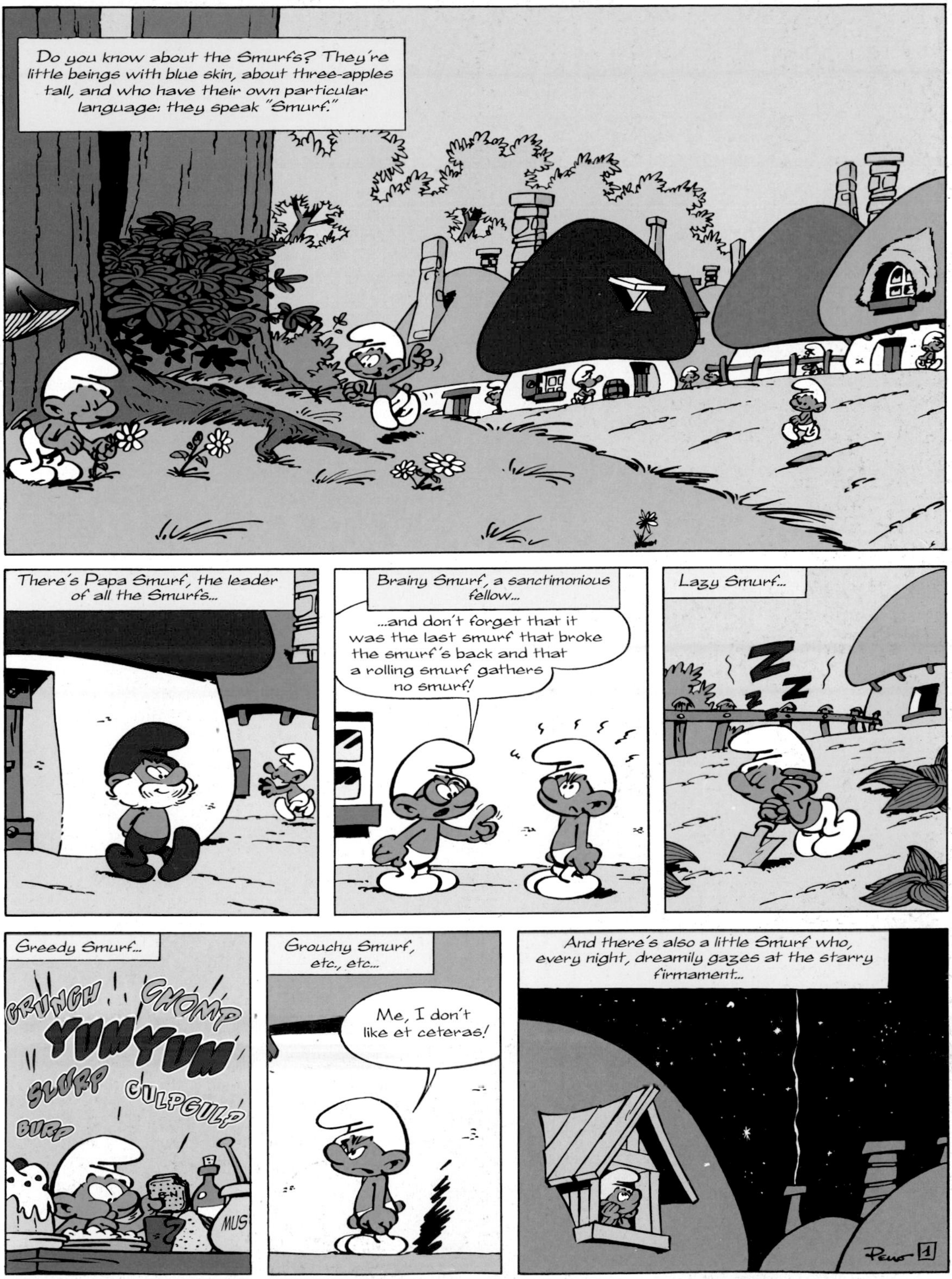

Do you know about the Smurfs? They're little beings with blue skin, about three-apples tall, and who have their own particular language: they speak "Smurf."
There's Papa Smurf, the leader of all the Smurfs...
Brainy Smurf, a sanctimonious fellow...
...and don't forget that it was the last smurf that broke the smurf's back and that a rolling smurf gathers no smurf!
Lazy Smurf...
ZZZ
Greedy Smurf...
CRUNCH
CHOMP
YUMYUM
SLURP
GULPGULP
BURP
MUS
Grouchy Smurf, etc., etc...
Me, I don't like et ceteras!
And there's also a little Smurf who, every night, dreamily gazes at the starry firmament...
Peyo
1

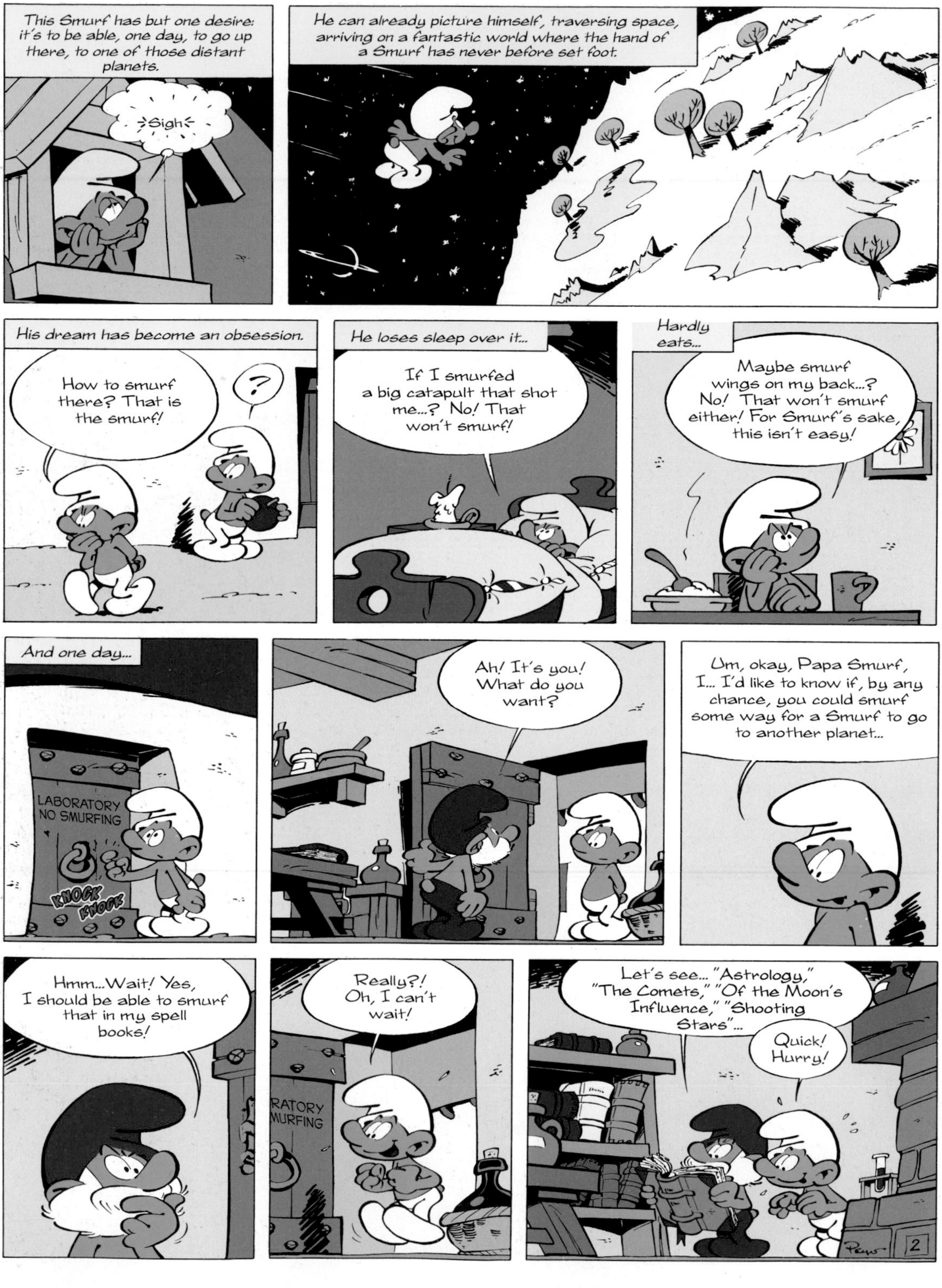
This Smurf has but one desire: it's to be able, one day, to go up there, to one of those distant planets.
Sigh
He can already picture himself, traversing space, arriving on a fantastic world where the hand of a Smurf has never before set foot.
His dream has become an obsession.
How to smurf there? That is the smurf!
?
He loses sleep over it...
If I smurfed a big catapult that shot me...? No! That won't smurf!
Hardly eats...
Maybe smurf wings on my back...? No! That won't smurf either! For Smurf's sake, this isn't easy!
And one day...
LABORATORY NO SMURFING
KNOCK KNOCK
Ah! It's you! What do you want?
Um, okay, Papa Smurf, I... I'd like to know if, by any chance, you could smurf some way for a Smurf to go to another planet...
Hmm...Wait! Yes, I should be able to smurf that in my spell books!
Really?! Oh, I can't wait!
RATORY SMURFING
Let's see... "Astrology," "The Comets," "Of the Moon's Influence," "Shooting Stars"...
Quick! Hurry!
Peyo
2

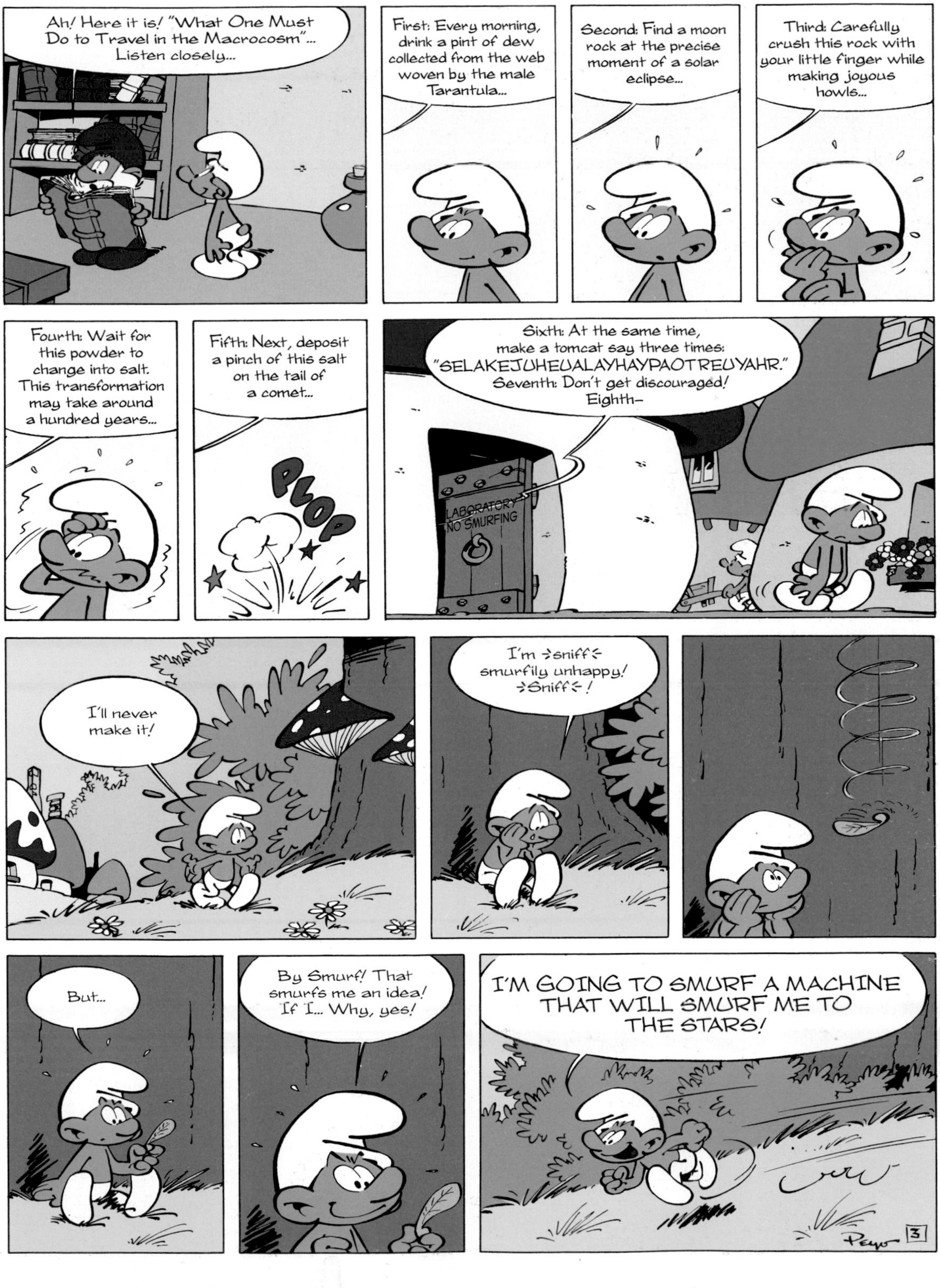

Ah! Here it is! "What One Must Do to Travel in the Macrocosm"... Listen closely...
First: Every morning, drink a pint of dew collected from the web woven by the male Tarantula...
Second: Find a moon rock at the precise moment of a solar eclipse...
Third: Carefully crush this rock with your little finger while making joyous howls...
Fourth: Wait for this powder to change into salt. This transformation may take around a hundred years...
Fifth: Next, deposit a pinch of this salt on the tail of a comet...
PLOP
Sixth: At the same time, make a tomcat say three times: "SELAKEJUHEUALAYHAYPAOTREUYAHR." Seventh: Don't get discouraged! Eighth–
LABORATORY NO SMURFING
I'll never make it!
I'm ⇝sniff⇜ smurfily unhappy! ⇝Sniff⇜!
But...
By Smurf! That smurfs me an idea! If I... Why, yes!
I'M GOING TO SMURF A MACHINE THAT WILL SMURF ME TO THE STARS!
Peyo 3

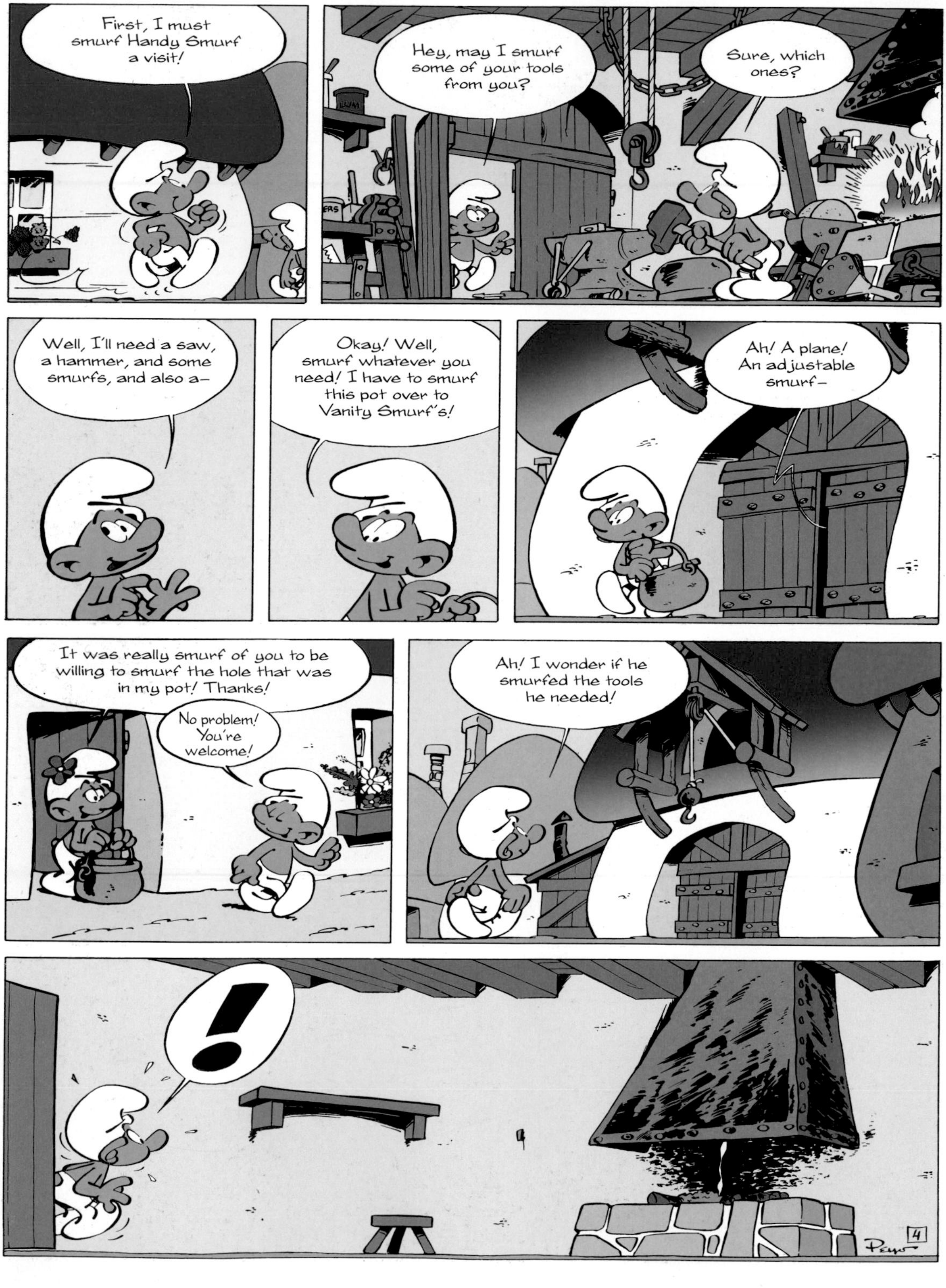
First, I must smurf Handy Smurf a visit!
Hey, may I smurf some of your tools from you?
Sure, which ones?
Well, I'll need a saw, a hammer, and some smurfs, and also a–
Okay! Well, smurf whatever you need! I have to smurf this pot over to Vanity Smurf's!
Ah! A plane! An adjustable smurf–
It was really smurf of you to be willing to smurf the hole that was in my pot! Thanks!
No problem! You're welcome!
Ah! I wonder if he smurfed the tools he needed!
!
4
Peyo

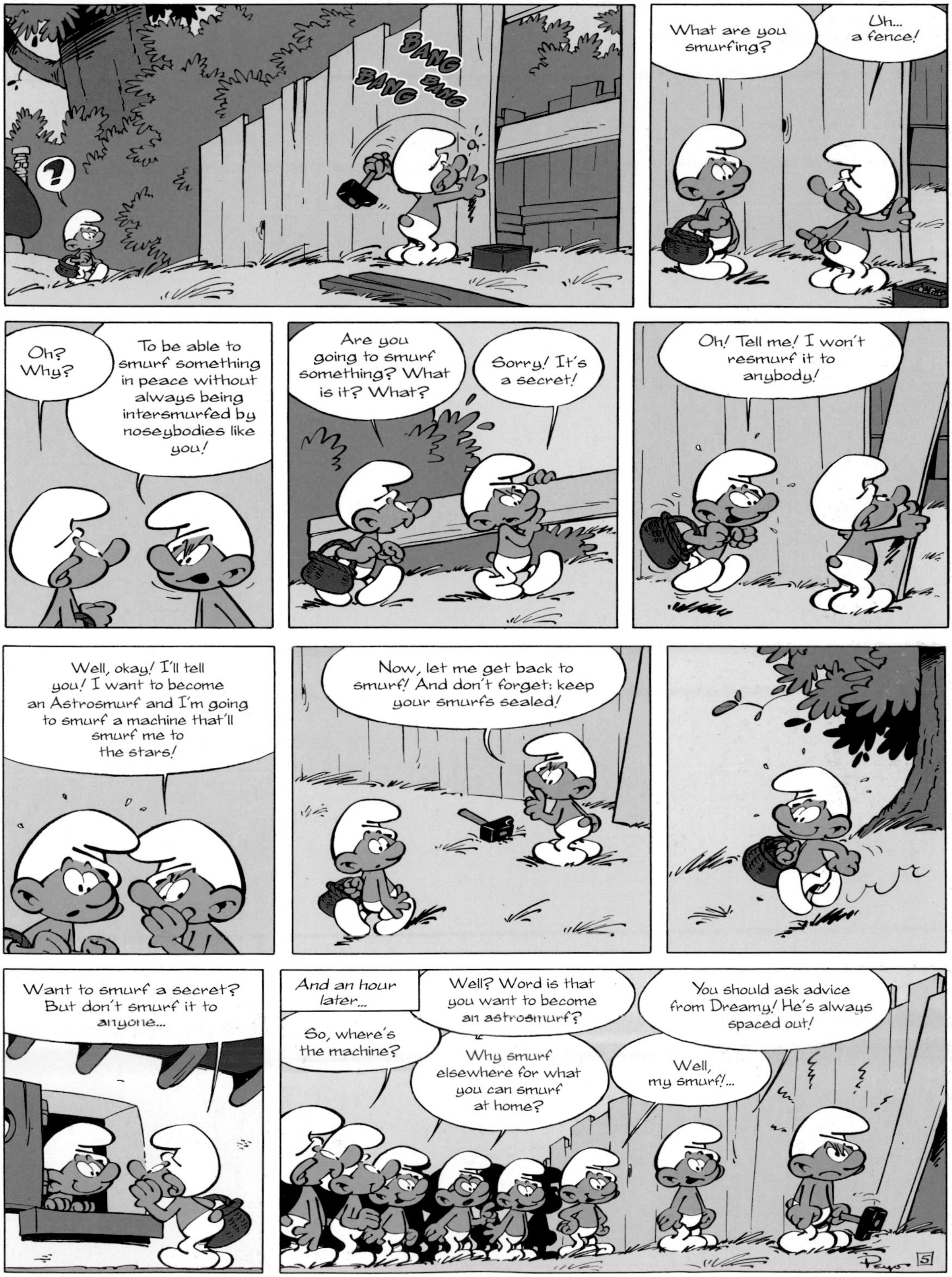
BANG BANG BANG
?
What are you smurfing?
Uh... a fence!
Oh? Why?
To be able to smurf something in peace without always being intersmurfed by noseybodies like you!
Are you going to smurf something? What is it? What?
Sorry! It's a secret!
Oh! Tell me! I won't resmurf it to anybody!
Well, okay! I'll tell you! I want to become an Astrosmurf and I'm going to smurf a machine that'll smurf me to the stars!
Now, let me get back to smurf! And don't forget: keep your smurfs sealed!
Want to smurf a secret? But don't smurf it to anyone...
And an hour later...
So, where's the machine?
Well? Word is that you want to become an astrosmurf?
Why smurf elsewhere for what you can smurf at home?
You should ask advice from Dreamy! He's always spaced out!
Well, my smurf!...
5

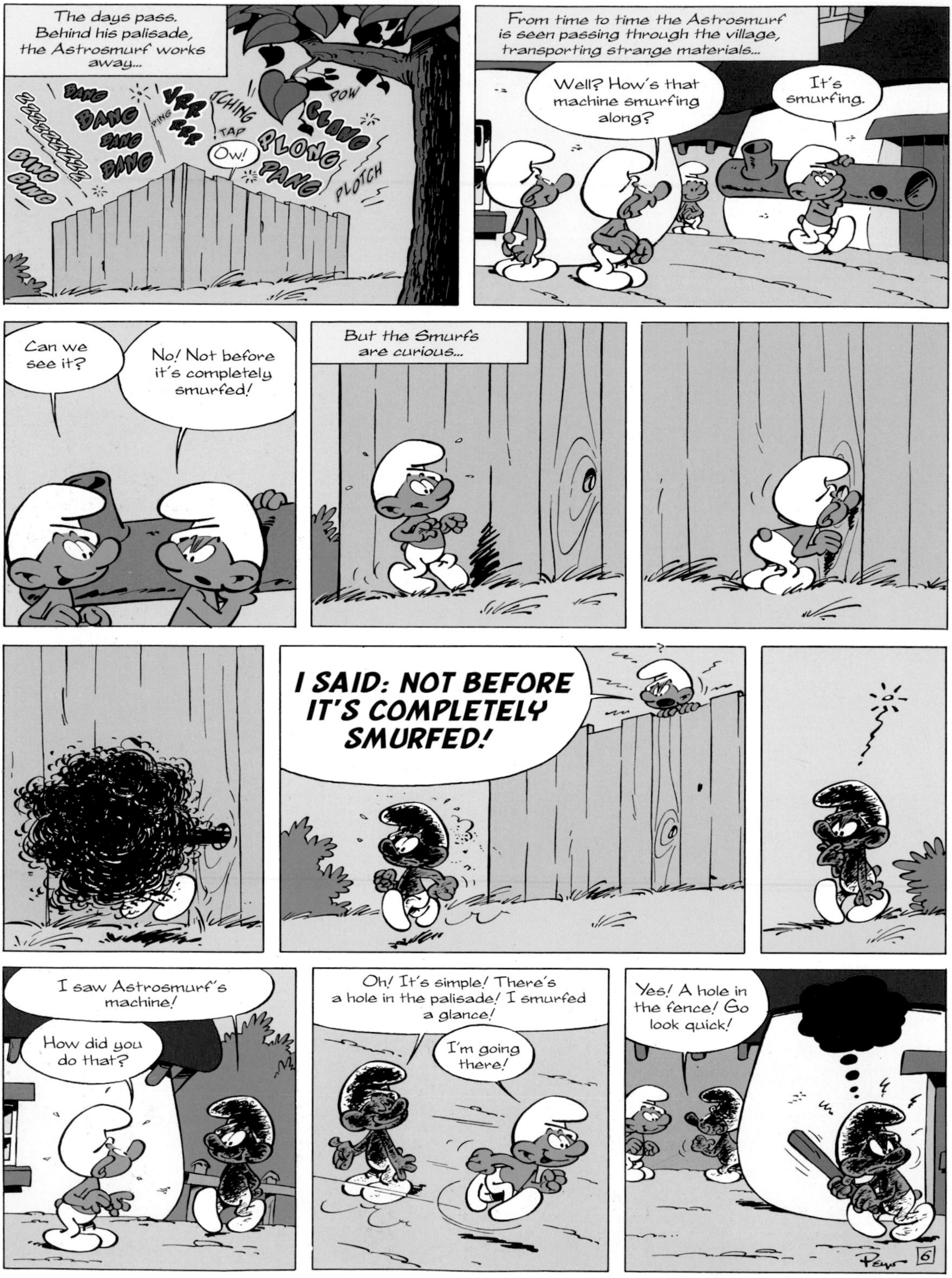
The days pass. Behind his palisade, the Astrosmurf works away...
BANG
BANG
BANG
BANG
VRR
RRR
PING
TCHING
TAP
Ow!
POW
CLANG
PLONG
PANG
PLOTCH
From time to time the Astrosmurf is seen passing through the village, transporting strange materials...
Well? How's that machine smurfing along?
It's smurfing.
Can we see it?
No! Not before it's completely smurfed!
But the Smurfs are curious...
I SAID: NOT BEFORE IT'S COMPLETELY SMURFED!
I saw Astrosmurf's machine!
How did you do that?
Oh! It's simple! There's a hole in the palisade! I smurfed a glance!
I'm going there!
Yes! A hole in the fence! Go look quick!
6

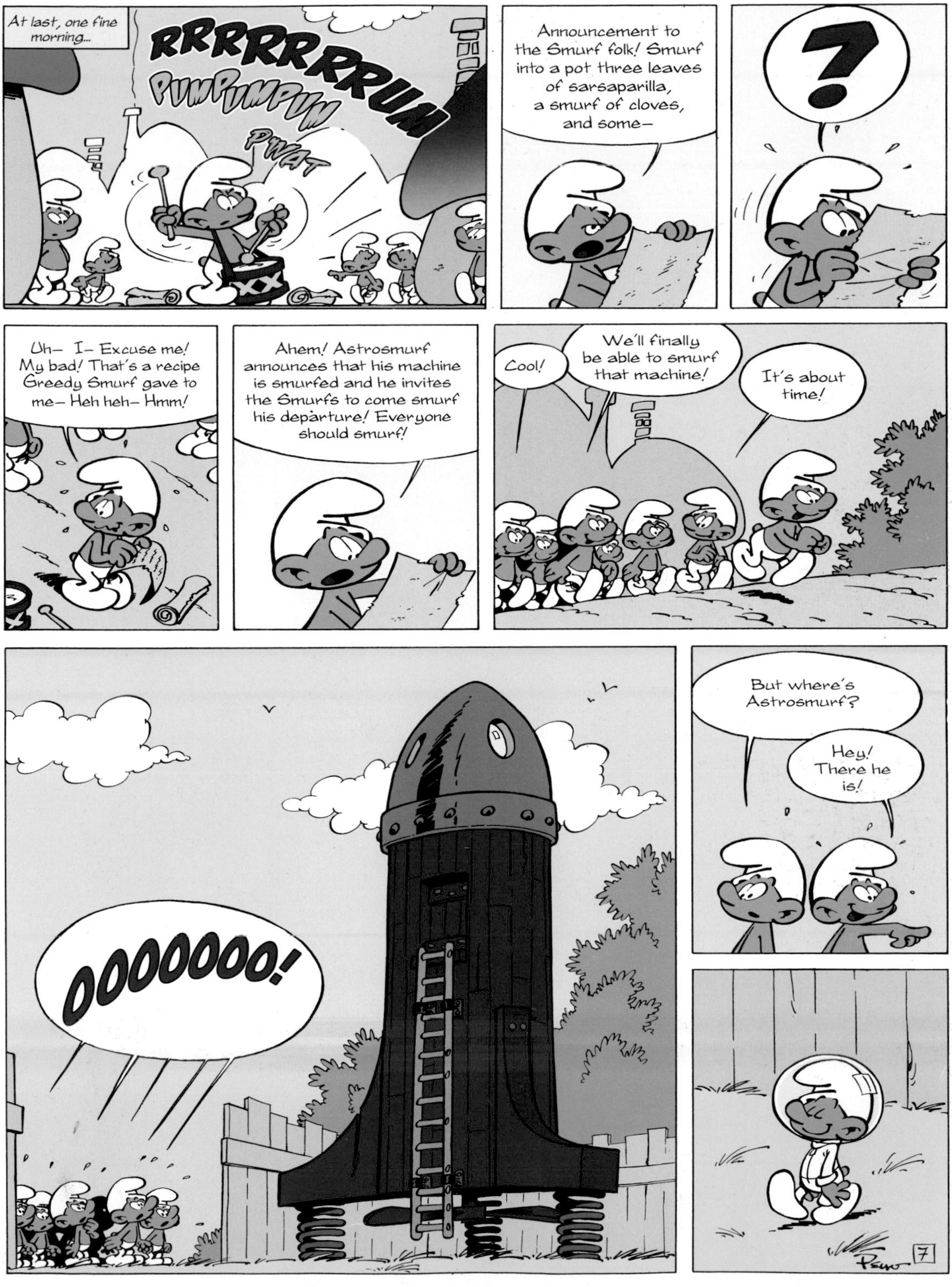

At last, one fine morning...
RRRRRRRRRUM
PUMPUMPUMPUM
PWAT
Announcement to the Smurf folk! Smurf into a pot three leaves of sarsaparilla, a smurf of cloves, and some—
?
Uh— I— Excuse me! My bad! That's a recipe Greedy Smurf gave to me— Heh heh— Hmm!
Ahem! Astrosmurf announces that his machine is smurfed and he invites the Smurfs to come smurf his departure! Everyone should smurf!
Cool!
We'll finally be able to smurf that machine!
It's about time!
OOOOOOO!
But where's Astrosmurf?
Hey! There he is!
7

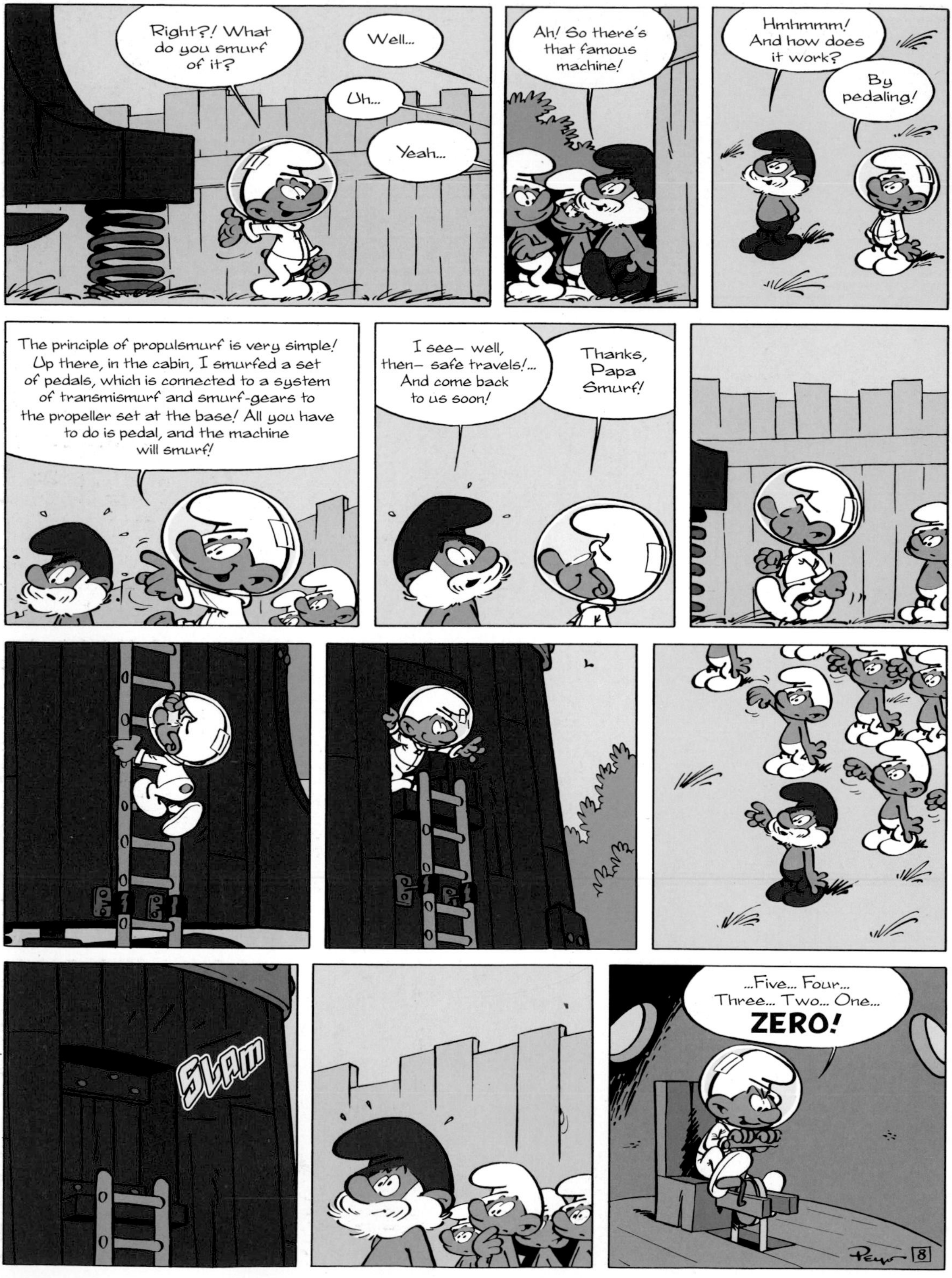
Right?! What do you smurf of it?
Well...
Uh...
Yeah...
Ah! So there's that famous machine!
Hmhmmm! And how does it work?
By pedaling!
The principle of propulsmurf is very simple! Up there, in the cabin, I smurfed a set of pedals, which is connected to a system of transmismurf and smurf-gears to the propeller set at the base! All you have to do is pedal, and the machine will smurf!
I see– well, then– safe travels!... And come back to us soon!
Thanks, Papa Smurf!
SLAM
...Five... Four... Three... Two... One... ZERO!
Peyo
8

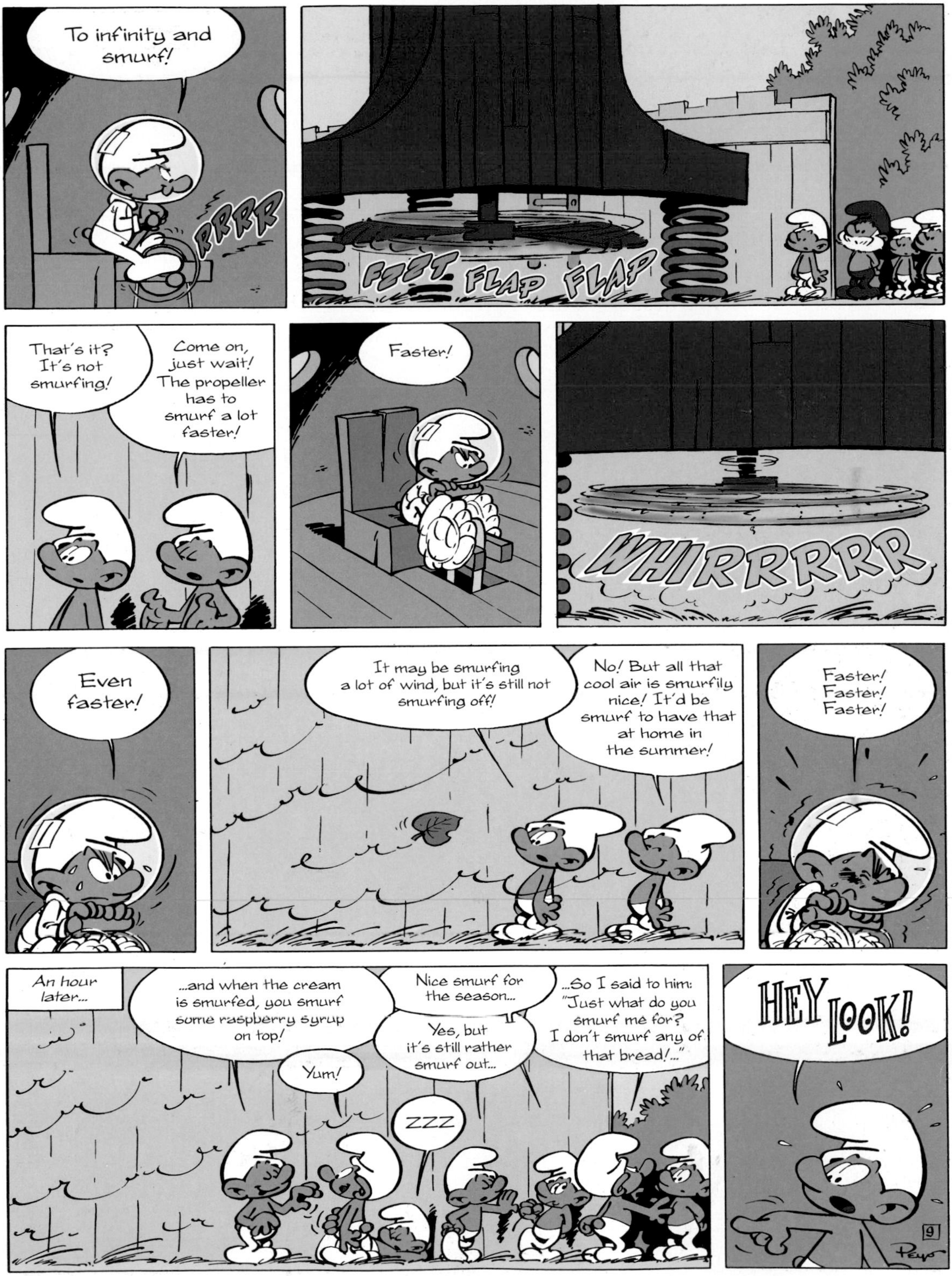
To infinity and smurf!
RRRR
FZZZT FLAP FLAP
That's it? It's not smurfing!
Come on, just wait! The propeller has to smurf a lot faster!
Faster!
WHIRRRRR
Even faster!
It may be smurfing a lot of wind, but it's still not smurfing off!
No! But all that cool air is smurfily nice! It'd be smurf to have that at home in the summer!
Faster! Faster! Faster!
An hour later...
...and when the cream is smurfed, you smurf some raspberry syrup on top!
Yum!
Nice smurf for the season...
Yes, but it's still rather smurf out...
ZZZ
...So I said to him: "Just what do you smurf me for? I don't smurf any of that bread!..."
HEY LOOK!
9
Peyo

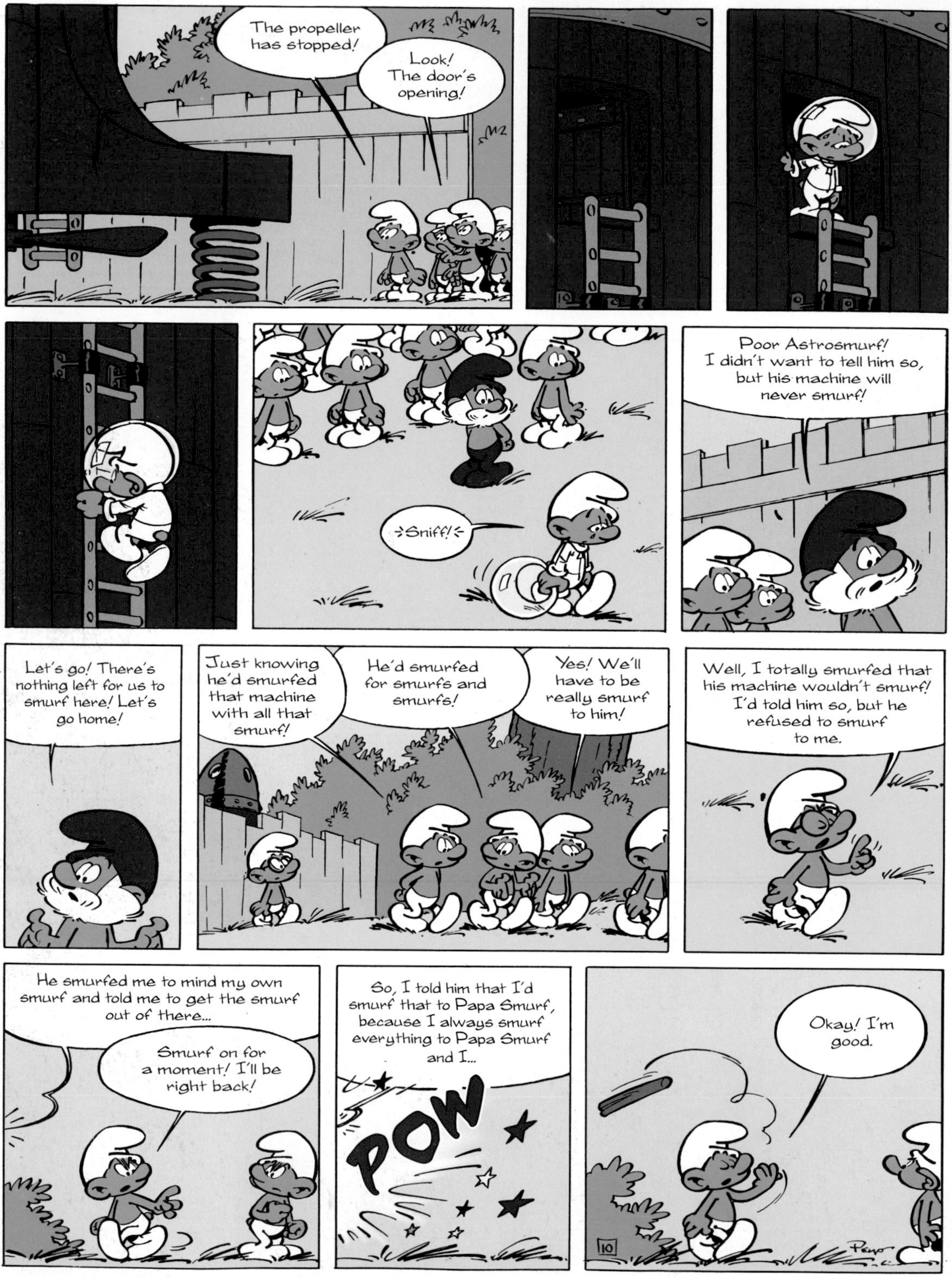
The propeller has stopped!
Look! The door's opening!
Poor Astrosmurf! I didn't want to tell him so, but his machine will never smurf!
Sniff!
Let's go! There's nothing left for us to smurf here! Let's go home!
Just knowing he'd smurfed that machine with all that smurf!
He'd smurfed for smurfs and smurfs!
Yes! We'll have to be really smurf to him!
Well, I totally smurfed that his machine wouldn't smurf! I'd told him so, but he refused to smurf to me.
He smurfed me to mind my own smurf and told me to get the smurf out of there...
Smurf on for a moment! I'll be right back!
So, I told him that I'd smurf that to Papa Smurf, because I always smurf everything to Papa Smurf and I...
POW
Okay! I'm good.
10
Peyo

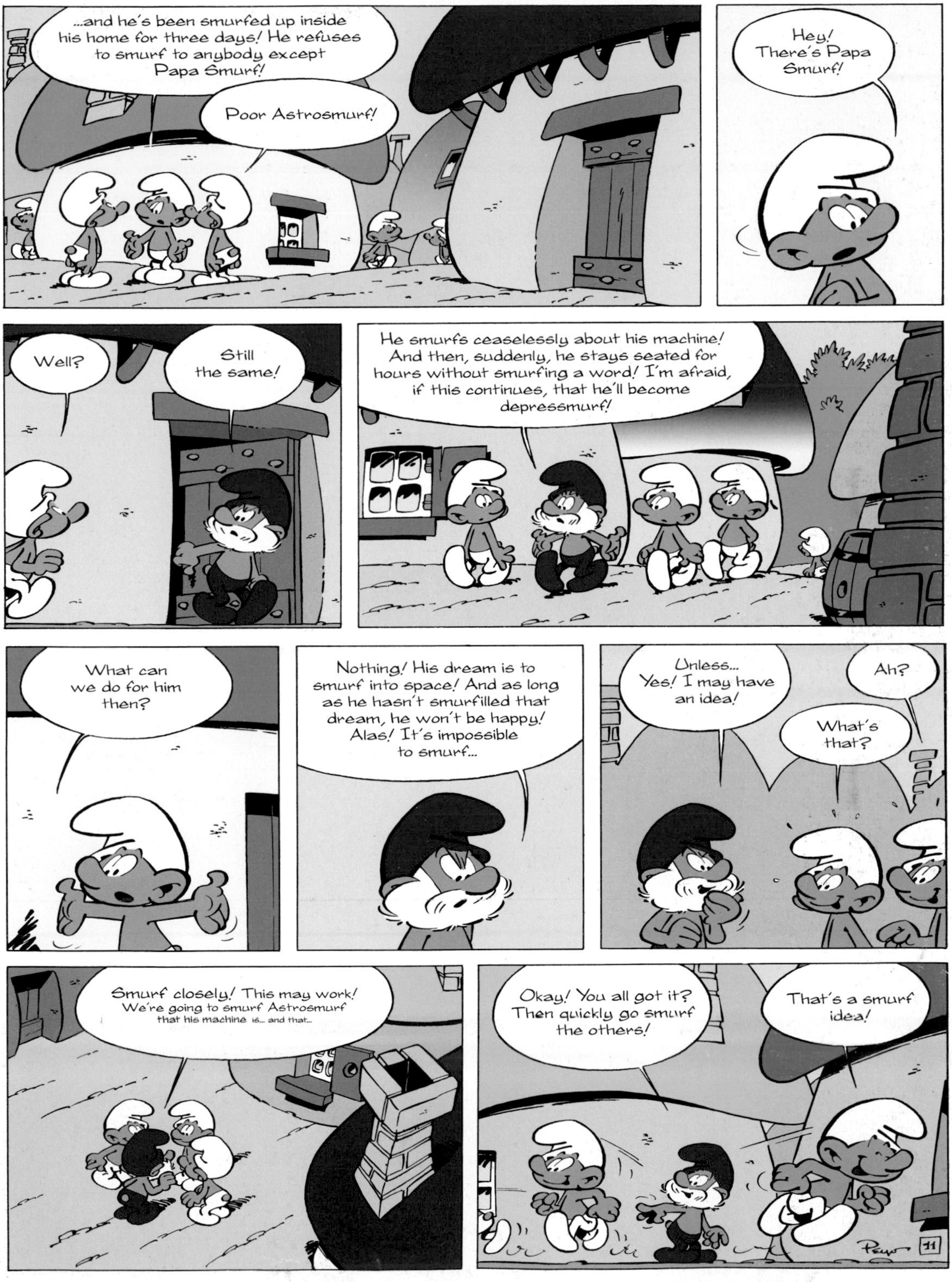
...and he's been smurfed up inside his home for three days! He refuses to smurf to anybody except Papa Smurf!
Poor Astrosmurf!
Hey! There's Papa Smurf!
Well?
Still the same!
He smurfs ceaselessly about his machine! And then, suddenly, he stays seated for hours without smurfing a word! I'm afraid, if this continues, that he'll become depressmurf!
What can we do for him then?
Nothing! His dream is to smurf into space! And as long as he hasn't smurfilled that dream, he won't be happy! Alas! It's impossible to smurf...
Unless... Yes! I may have an idea!
Ah?
What's that?
Smurf closely! This may work! We're going to smurf Astrosmurf that his machine is... and that...
Okay! You all got it? Then quickly go smurf the others!
That's a smurf idea!

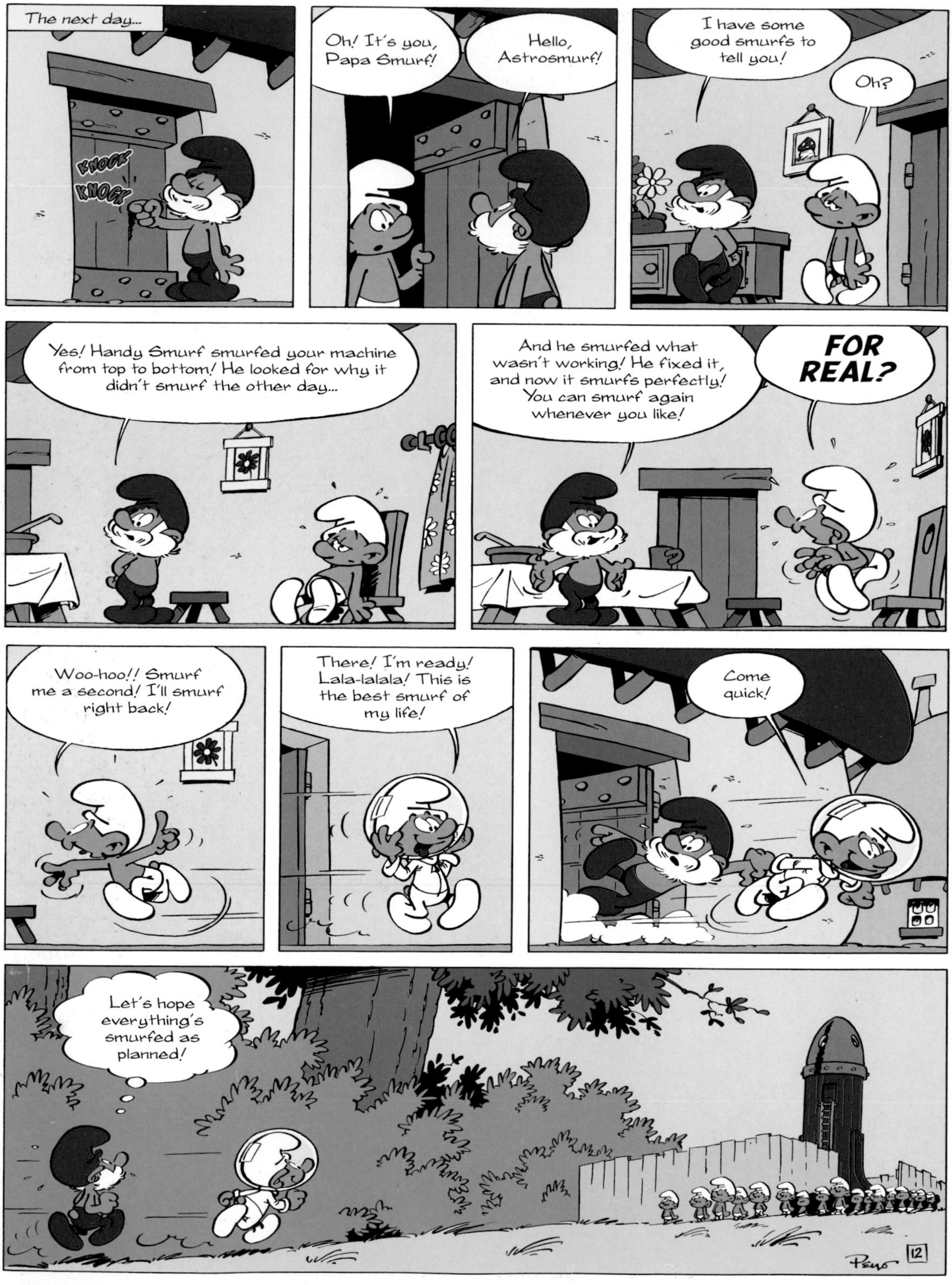

The next day...
KNOCK
KNOCK
Oh! It's you, Papa Smurf!
Hello, Astrosmurf!
I have some good smurfs to tell you!
Oh?
Yes! Handy Smurf smurfed your machine from top to bottom! He looked for why it didn't smurf the other day...
And he smurfed what wasn't working! He fixed it, and now it smurfs perfectly! You can smurf again whenever you like!
FOR REAL?
Woo-hoo!! Smurf me a second! I'll smurf right back!
There! I'm ready! Lala-lalala! This is the best smurf of my life!
Come quick!
Let's hope everything's smurfed as planned!
12

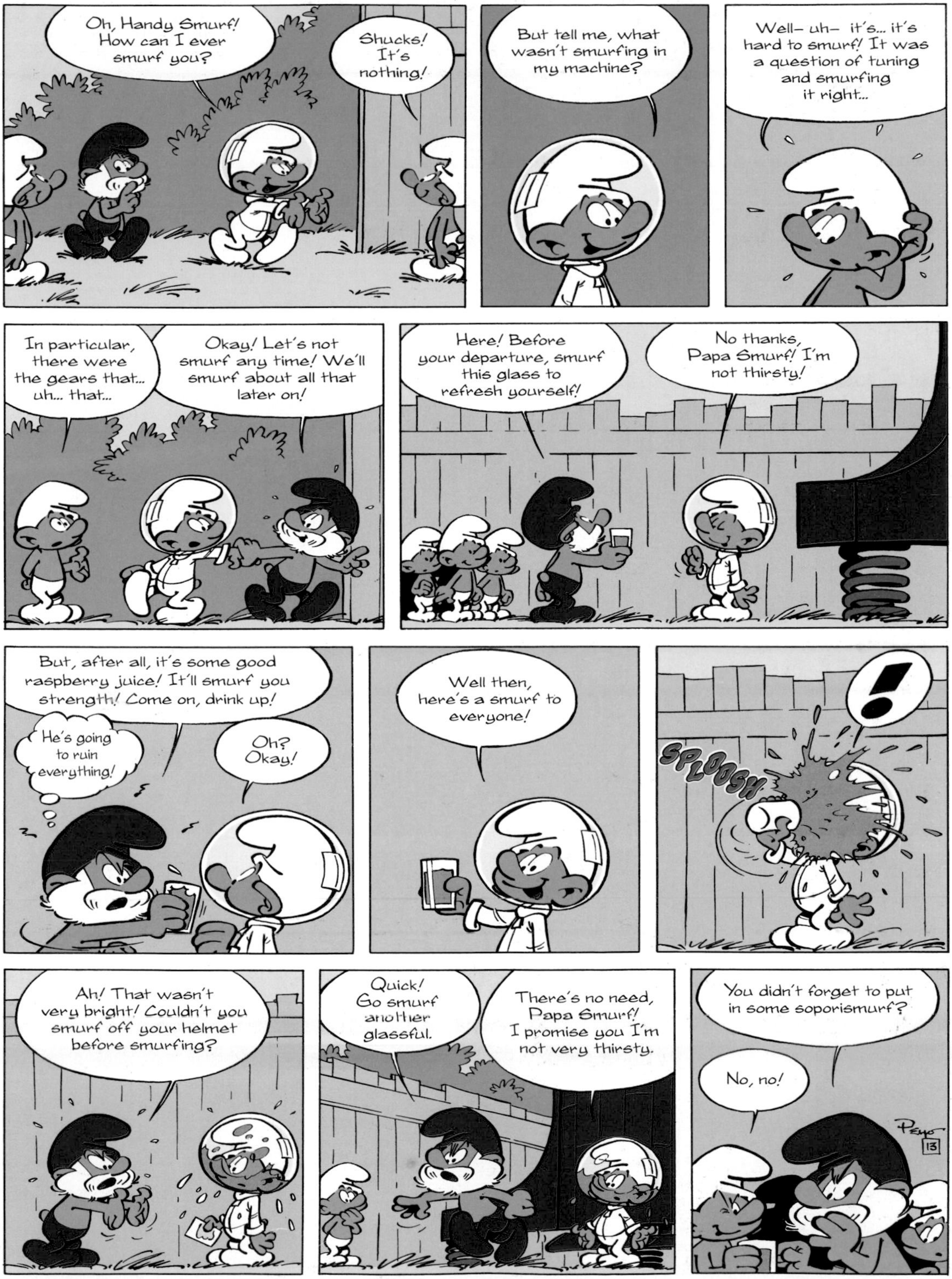

Oh, Handy Smurf! How can I ever smurf you?
Shucks! It's nothing!
But tell me, what wasn't smurfing in my machine?
Well– uh– it's... it's hard to smurf! It was a question of tuning and smurfing it right...
In particular, there were the gears that... uh... that...
Okay! Let's not smurf any time! We'll smurf about all that later on!
Here! Before your departure, smurf this glass to refresh yourself!
No thanks, Papa Smurf! I'm not thirsty!
But, after all, it's some good raspberry juice! It'll smurf you strength! Come on, drink up!
He's going to ruin everything!
Oh? Okay!
Well then, here's a smurf to everyone!
SPLOOSH
!
Ah! That wasn't very bright! Couldn't you smurf off your helmet before smurfing?
Quick! Go smurf another glassful.
There's no need, Papa Smurf! I promise you I'm not very thirsty.
You didn't forget to put in some soporismurf?
No, no!
Peyo
13

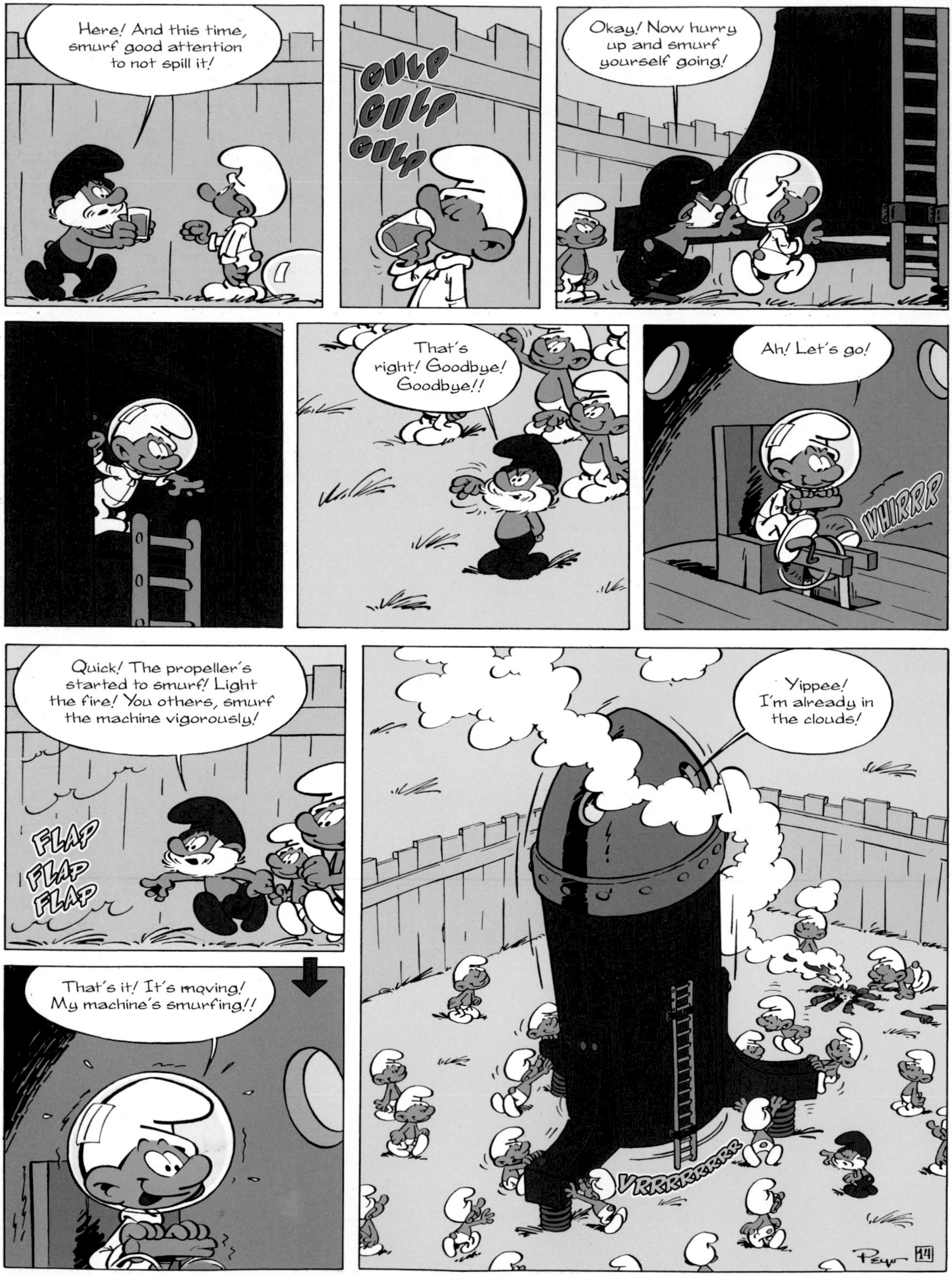
Here! And this time, smurf good attention to not spill it!
GULP GULP GULP
Okay! Now hurry up and smurf yourself going!
That's right! Goodbye! Goodbye!!
Ah! Let's go!
WHIRRR
Quick! The propeller's started to smurf! Light the fire! You others, smurf the machine vigorously!
FLAP FLAP FLAP
That's it! It's moving! My machine's smurfing!!
Yippee! I'm already in the clouds!
VRRRRRRRR
Peyo
14

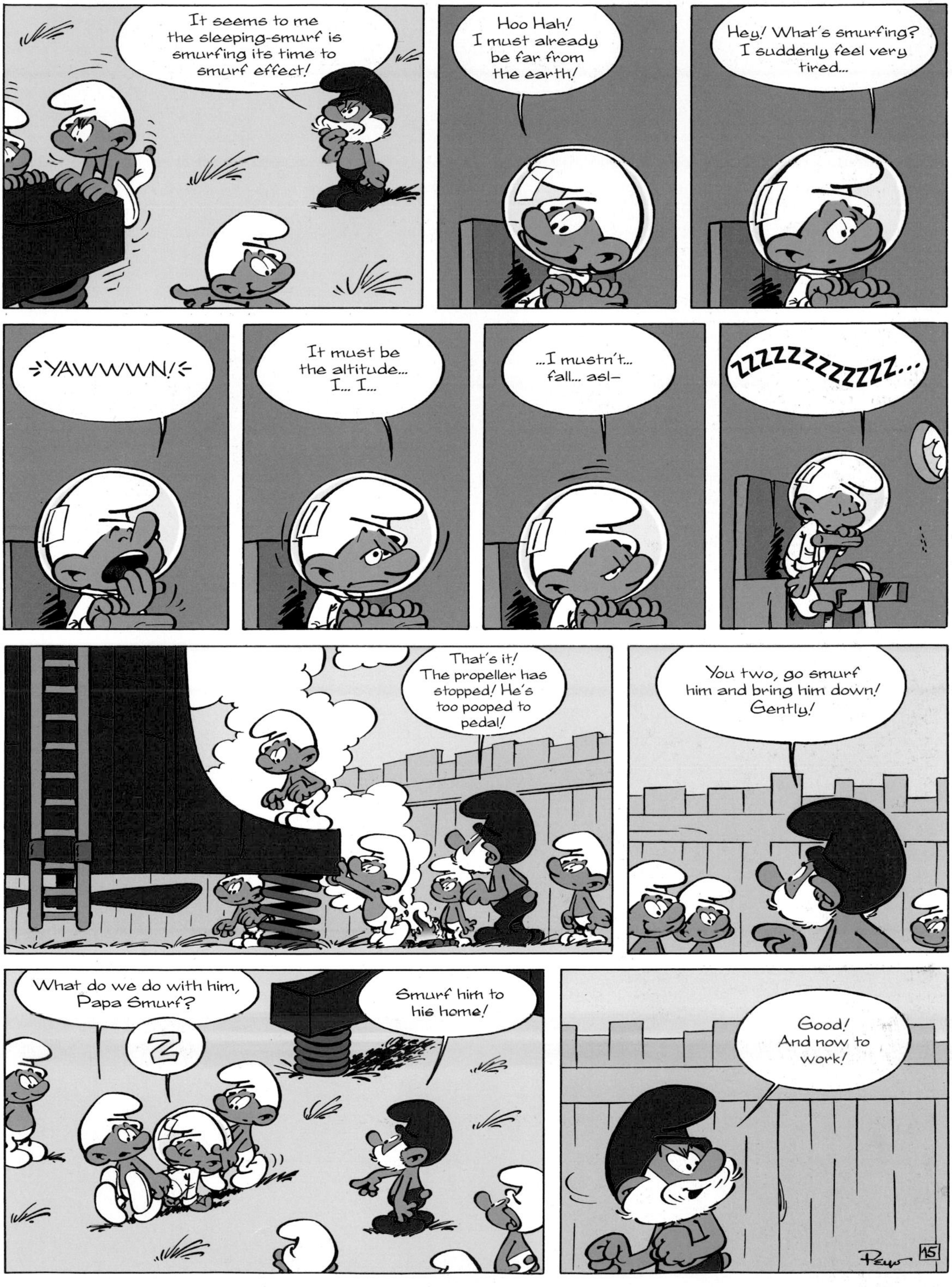
It seems to me the sleeping-smurf is smurfing its time to smurf effect!
Hoo Hah! I must already be far from the earth!
Hey! What's smurfing? I suddenly feel very tired...
YAWWWN!
It must be the altitude... I... I...
...I mustn't... fall... asl–
ZZZZZZZZZZZ...
That's it! The propeller has stopped! He's too pooped to pedal!
You two, go smurf him and bring him down! Gently!
What do we do with him, Papa Smurf?
Z
Smurf him to his home!
Good! And now to work!
Peyo
15

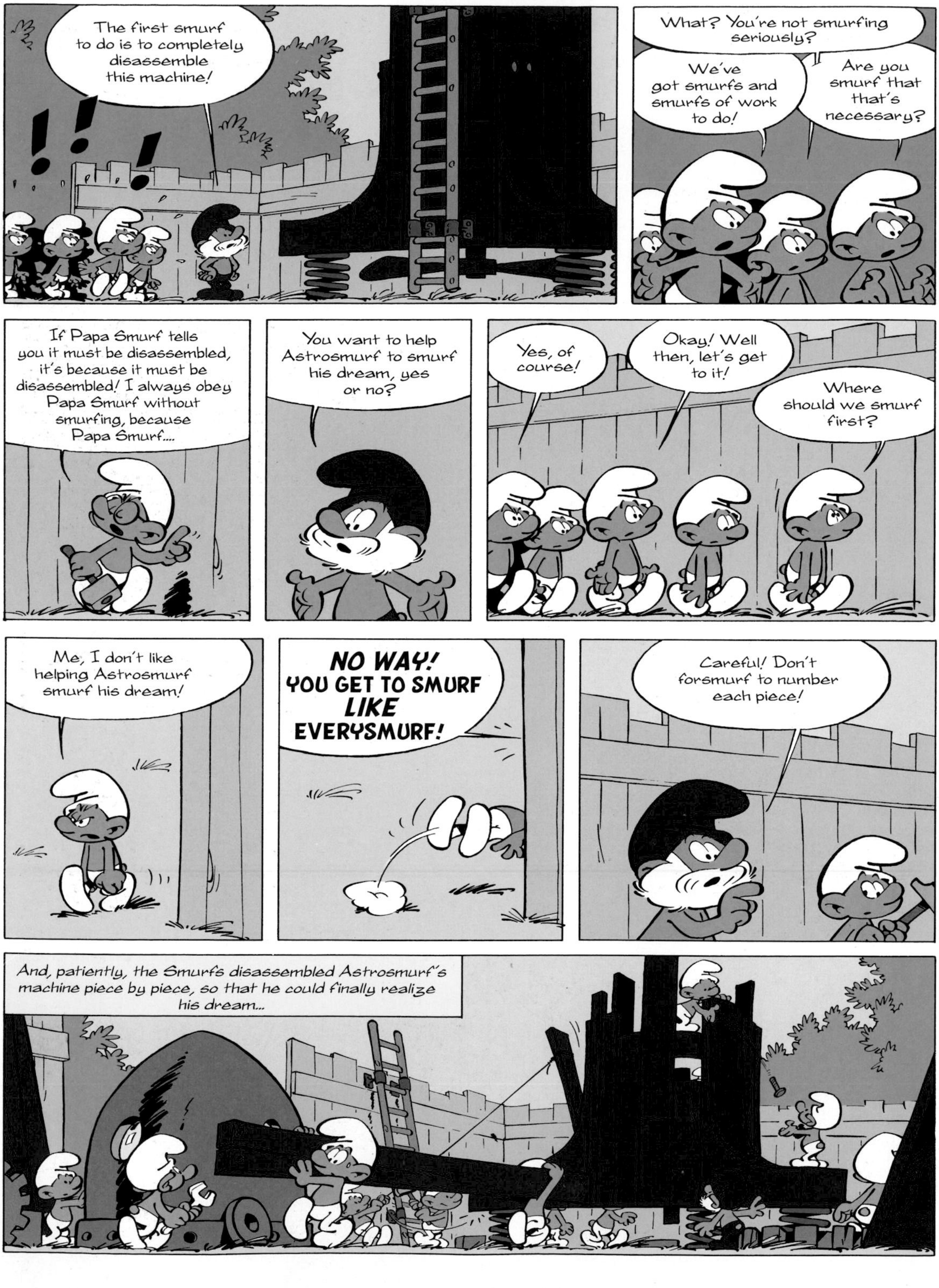

The first smurf to do is to completely disassemble this machine!
!
!
!
What? You're not smurfing seriously?
We've got smurfs and smurfs of work to do!
Are you smurf that that's necessary?
If Papa Smurf tells you it must be disassembled, it's because it must be disassembled! I always obey Papa Smurf without smurfing, because Papa Smurf....
You want to help Astrosmurf to smurf his dream, yes or no?
Yes, of course!
Okay! Well then, let's get to it!
Where should we smurf first?
Me, I don't like helping Astrosmurf smurf his dream!
NO WAY! YOU GET TO SMURF LIKE EVERYSMURF!
Careful! Don't forsmurf to number each piece!
And, patiently, the Smurfs disassembled Astrosmurf's machine piece by piece, so that he could finally realize his dream...

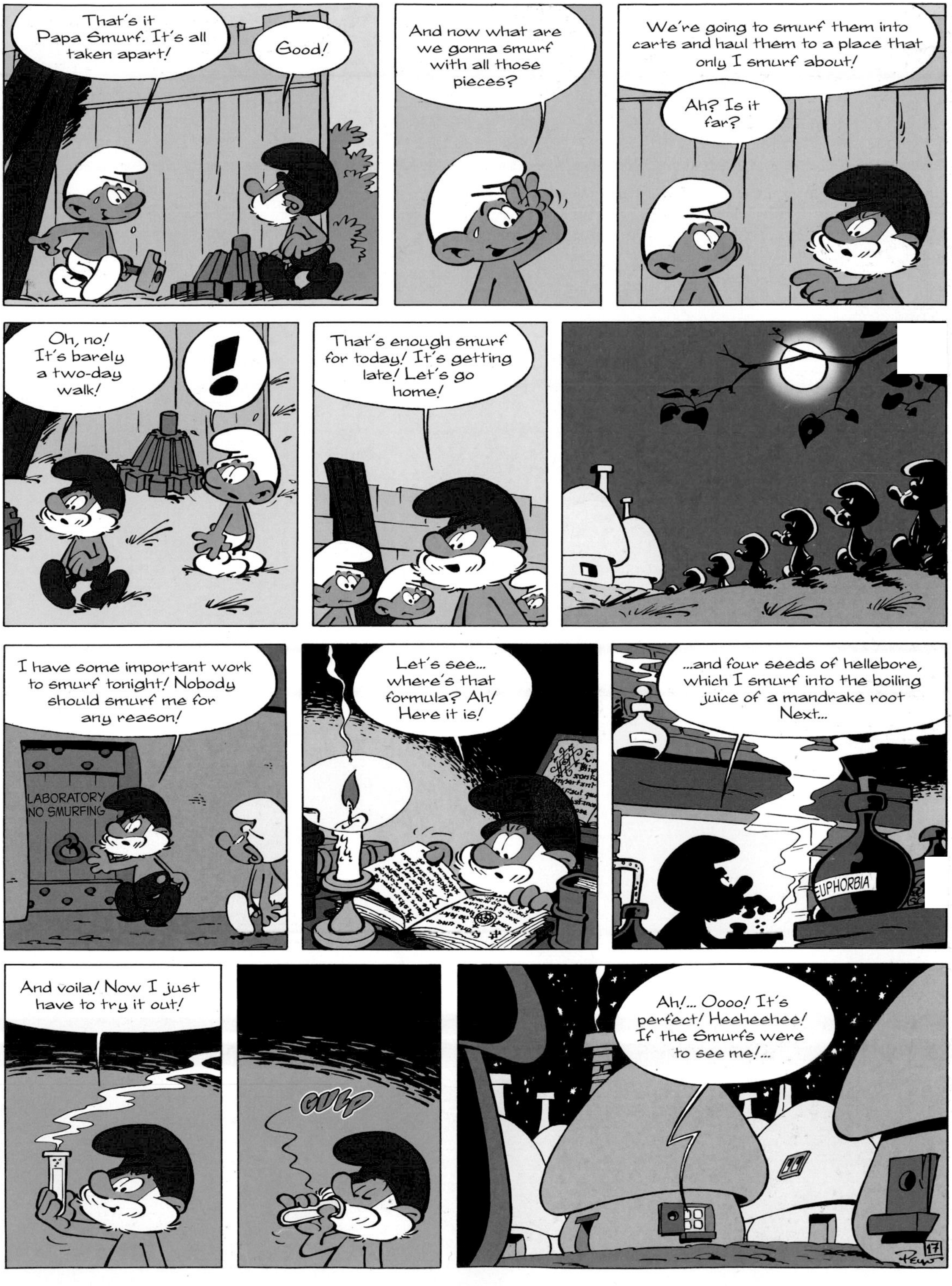

That's it Papa Smurf. It's all taken apart!
Good!
And now what are we gonna smurf with all those pieces?
We're going to smurf them into carts and haul them to a place that only I smurf about!
Ah? Is it far?
Oh, no! It's barely a two-day walk!
!
That's enough smurf for today! It's getting late! Let's go home!
I have some important work to smurf tonight! Nobody should smurf me for any reason!
LABORATORY NO SMURFING
Let's see... where's that formula? Ah! Here it is!
...and four seeds of hellebore, which I smurf into the boiling juice of a mandrake root Next...
EUPHORBIA
And voila! Now I just have to try it out!
GULP
Ah!... Oooo! It's perfect! Heeheehee! If the Smurfs were to see me!...
17

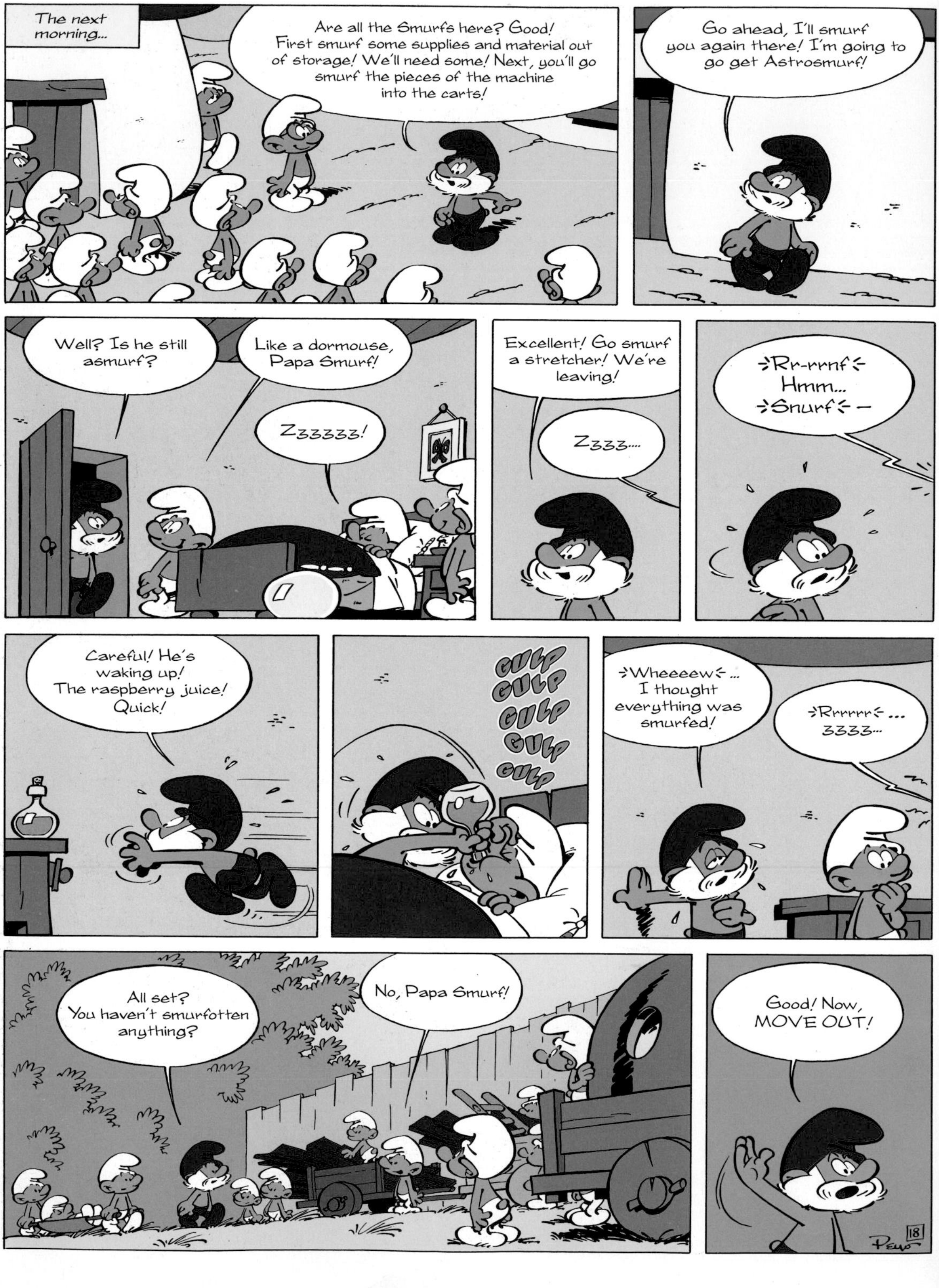
The next morning...
Are all the Smurfs here? Good! First smurf some supplies and material out of storage! We'll need some! Next, you'll go smurf the pieces of the machine into the carts!
Go ahead, I'll smurf you again there! I'm going to go get Astrosmurf!
Well? Is he still asmurf?
Like a dormouse, Papa Smurf!
Z33333!
Excellent! Go smurf a stretcher! We're leaving!
Z333....
Rr-rrnf Hmm... Snurf –
Careful! He's waking up! The raspberry juice! Quick!
GULP GULP GULP GULP GULP
Wheeeew... I thought everything was smurfed!
Rrrrrr... 3333...
All set? You haven't smurfotten anything?
No, Papa Smurf!
Good! Now, MOVE OUT!
18

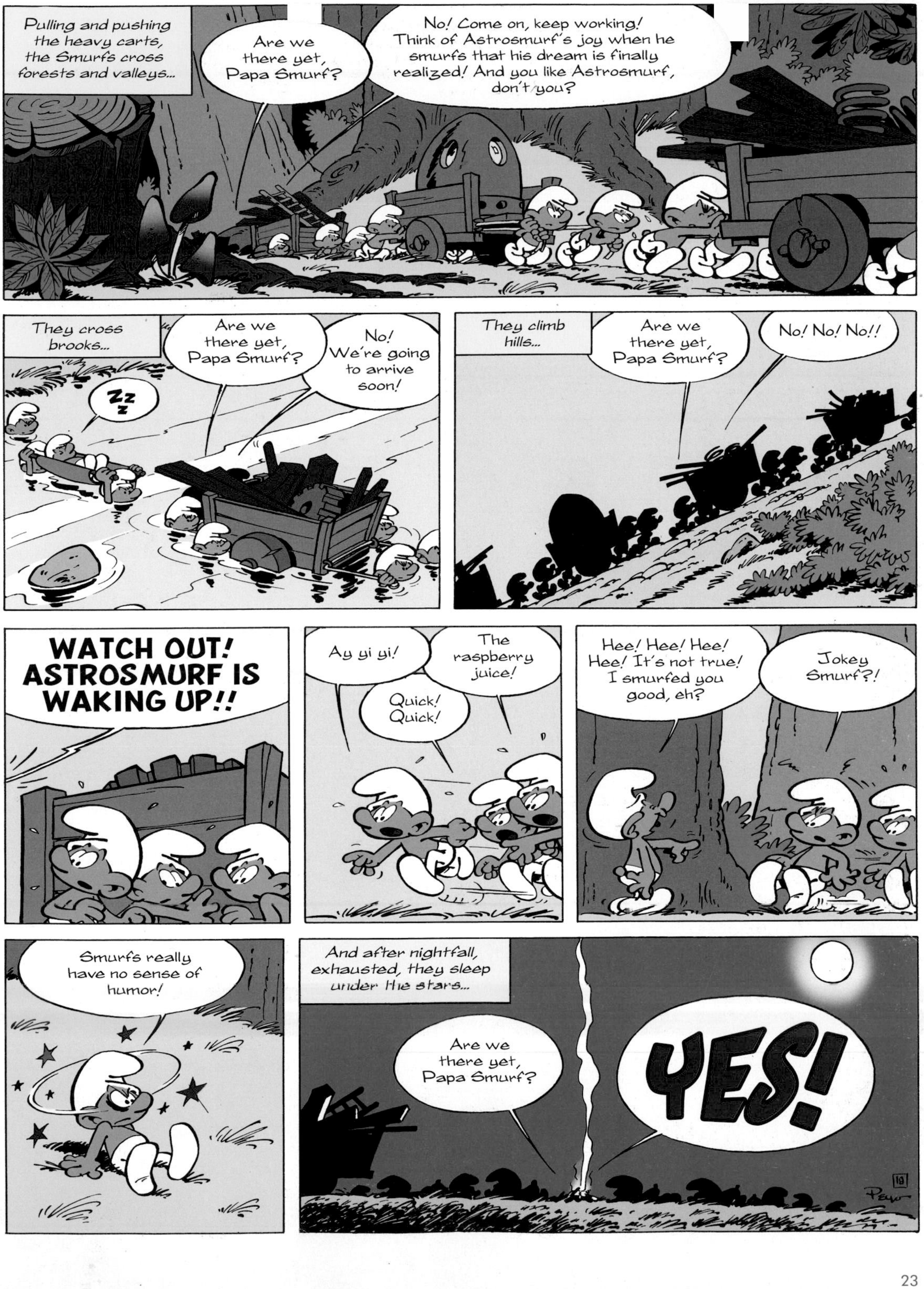
Pulling and pushing the heavy carts, the Smurfs cross forests and valleys...
Are we there yet, Papa Smurf?
No! Come on, keep working! Think of Astrosmurf's joy when he smurfs that his dream is finally realized! And you like Astrosmurf, don't you?
They cross brooks...
ZZ Z
Are we there yet, Papa Smurf?
No! We're going to arrive soon!
They climb hills...
Are we there yet, Papa Smurf?
No! No! No!!
WATCH OUT! ASTROSMURF IS WAKING UP!!
Ay yi yi!
The raspberry juice!
Quick! Quick!
Hee! Hee! Hee! Hee! It's not true! I smurfed you good, eh?
Jokey Smurf?!
Smurfs really have no sense of humor!
And after nightfall, exhausted, they sleep under the stars...
Are we there yet, Papa Smurf?
YES!

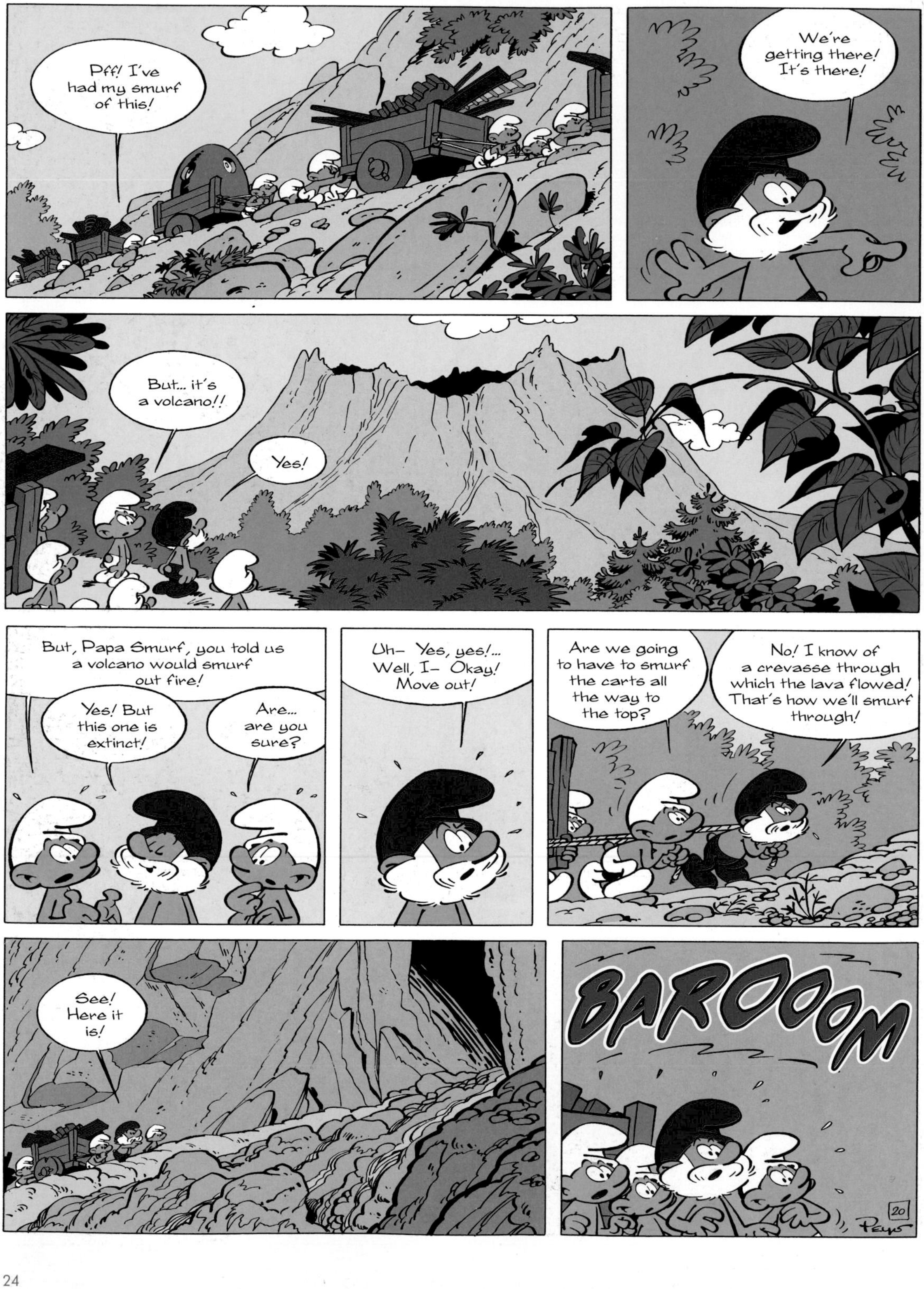

Pff! I've had my smurf of this!
We're getting there! It's there!
But... it's a volcano!!
Yes!
But, Papa Smurf, you told us a volcano would smurf out fire!
Yes! But this one is extinct!
Are... are you sure?
Uh- Yes, yes!... Well, I- Okay! Move out!
Are we going to have to smurf the carts all the way to the top?
No! I know of a crevasse through which the lava flowed! That's how we'll smurf through!
See! Here it is!
BAROOOM
20
Peyo

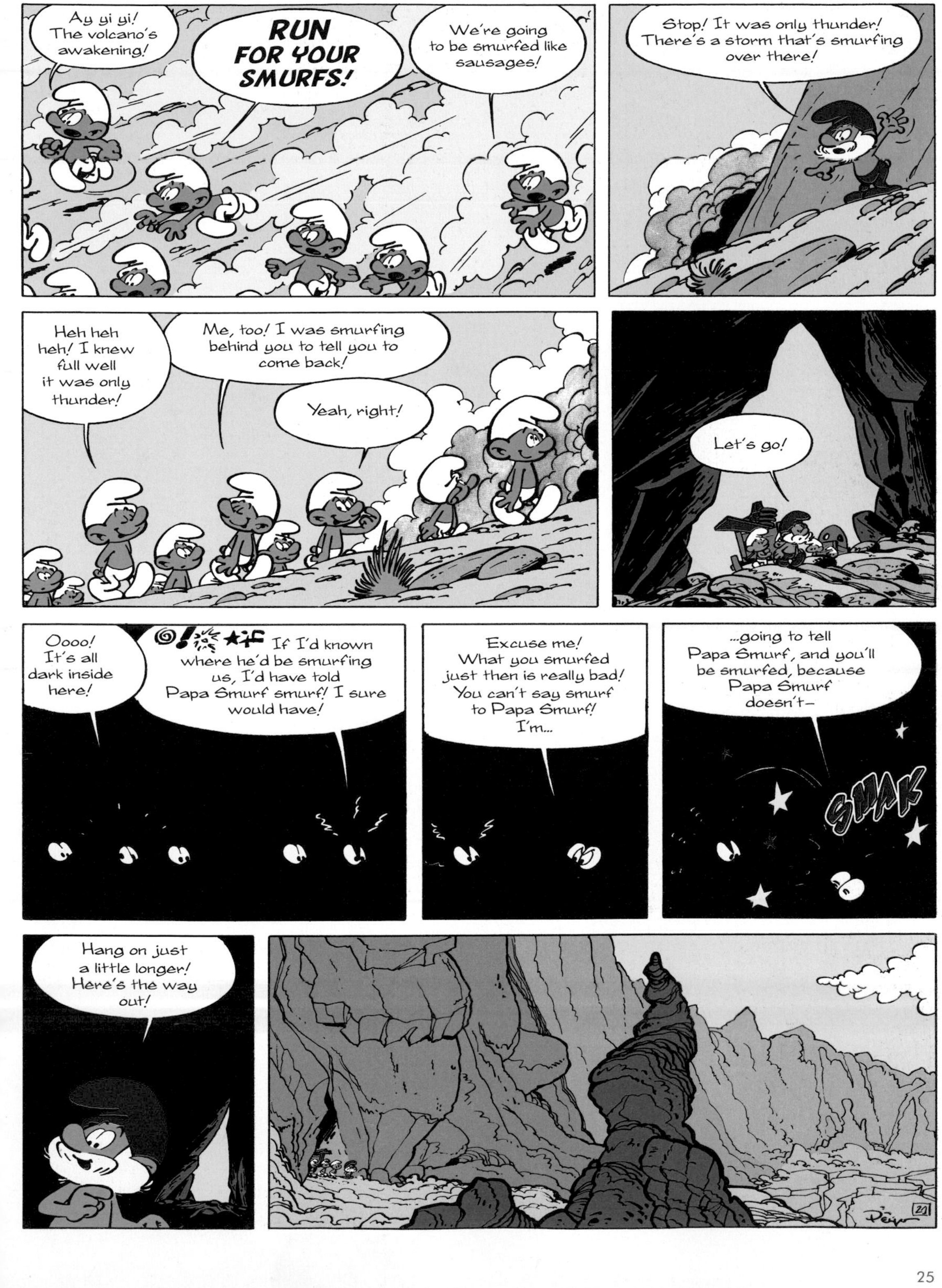
Ay yi yi! The volcano's awakening!
RUN FOR YOUR SMURFS!
We're going to be smurfed like sausages!
Stop! It was only thunder! There's a storm that's smurfing over there!
Heh heh heh! I knew full well it was only thunder!
Me, too! I was smurfing behind you to tell you to come back!
Yeah, right!
Let's go!
Oooo! It's all dark inside here!
If I'd known where he'd be smurfing us, I'd have told Papa Smurf smurf! I sure would have!
Excuse me! What you smurfed just then is really bad! You can't say smurf to Papa Smurf! I'm...
...going to tell Papa Smurf, and you'll be smurfed, because Papa Smurf doesn't–
SMAK
Hang on just a little longer! Here's the way out!

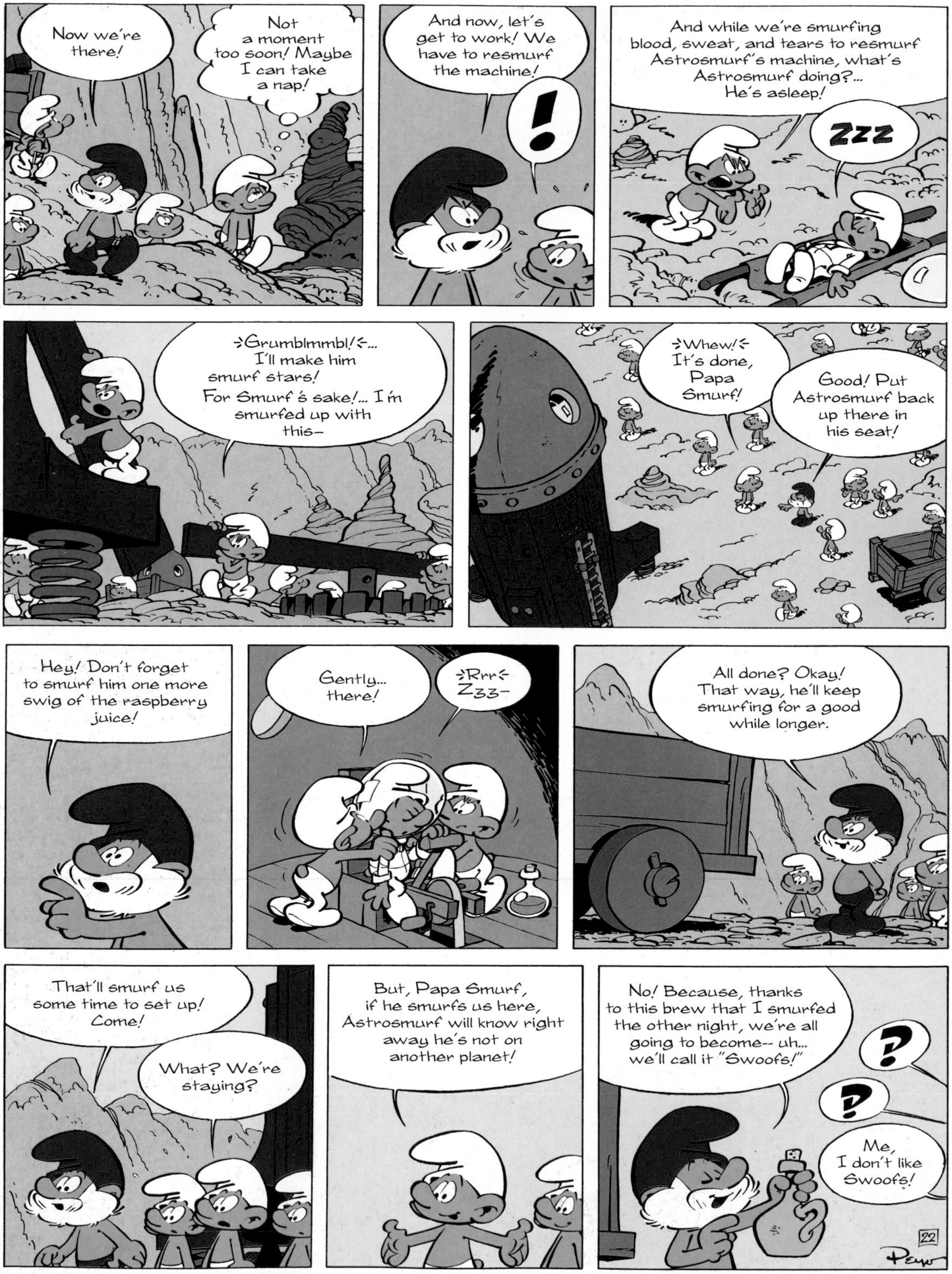

Now we're there!
Not a moment too soon! Maybe I can take a nap!
And now, let's get to work! We have to resmurf the machine!
!
And while we're smurfing blood, sweat, and tears to resmurf Astrosmurf's machine, what's Astrosmurf doing?... He's asleep!
ZZZ
Grumblmmbl!... I'll make him smurf stars! For Smurf's sake!... I'm smurfed up with this–
Whew! It's done, Papa Smurf!
Good! Put Astrosmurf back up there in his seat!
Hey! Don't forget to smurf him one more swig of the raspberry juice!
Gently... there!
Rrr Zzz–
All done? Okay! That way, he'll keep smurfing for a good while longer.
That'll smurf us some time to set up! Come!
What? We're staying?
But, Papa Smurf, if he smurfs us here, Astrosmurf will know right away he's not on another planet!
No! Because, thanks to this brew that I smurfed the other night, we're all going to become-- uh... we'll call it "Swoofs!"
?
?
Me, I don't like Swoofs!
22

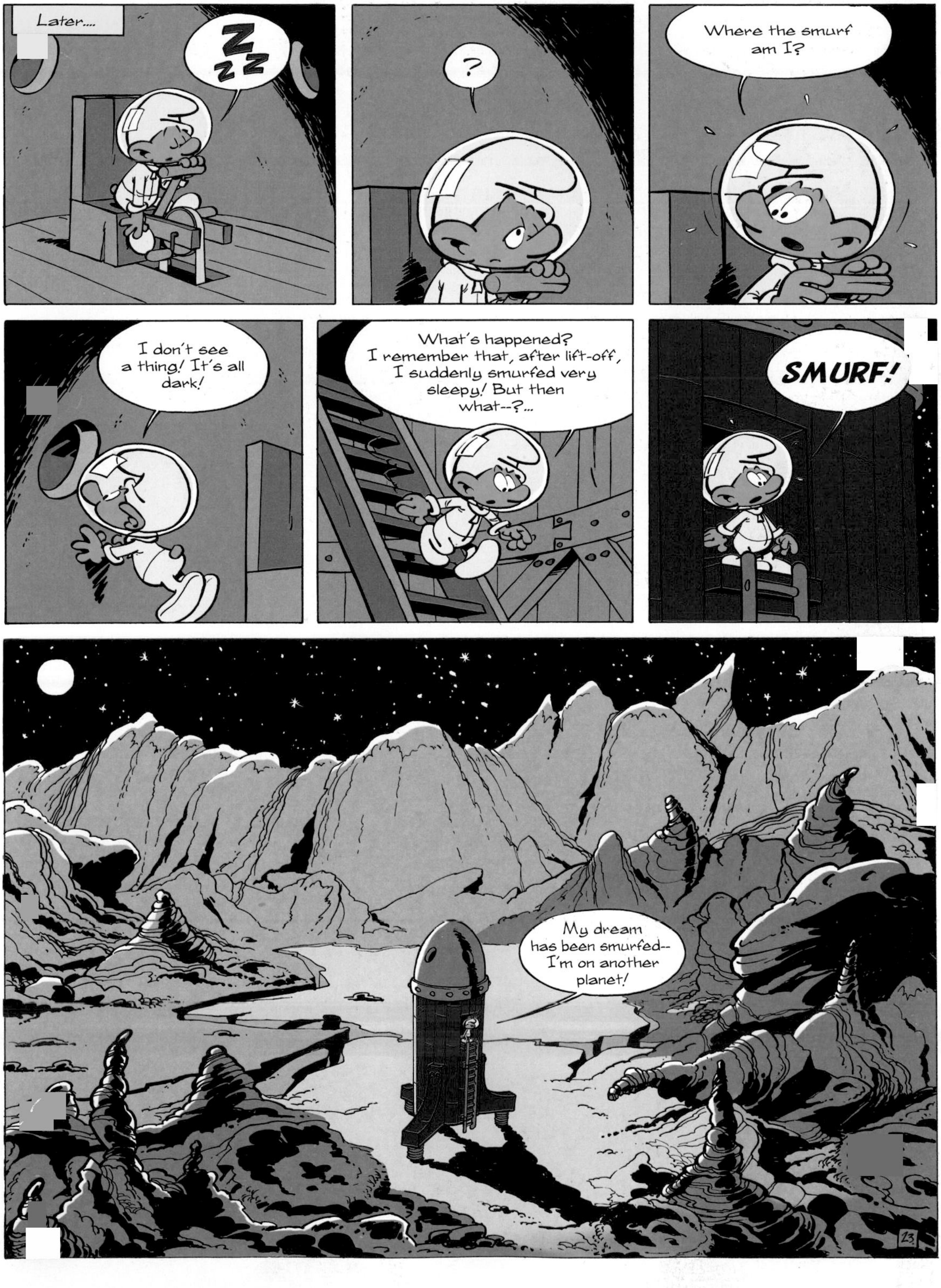

Later....
ZZZ
?
Where the smurf am I?
I don't see a thing! It's all dark!
What's happened? I remember that, after lift-off, I suddenly smurfed very sleepy! But then what--?...
SMURF!
My dream has been smurfed-- I'm on another planet!
23

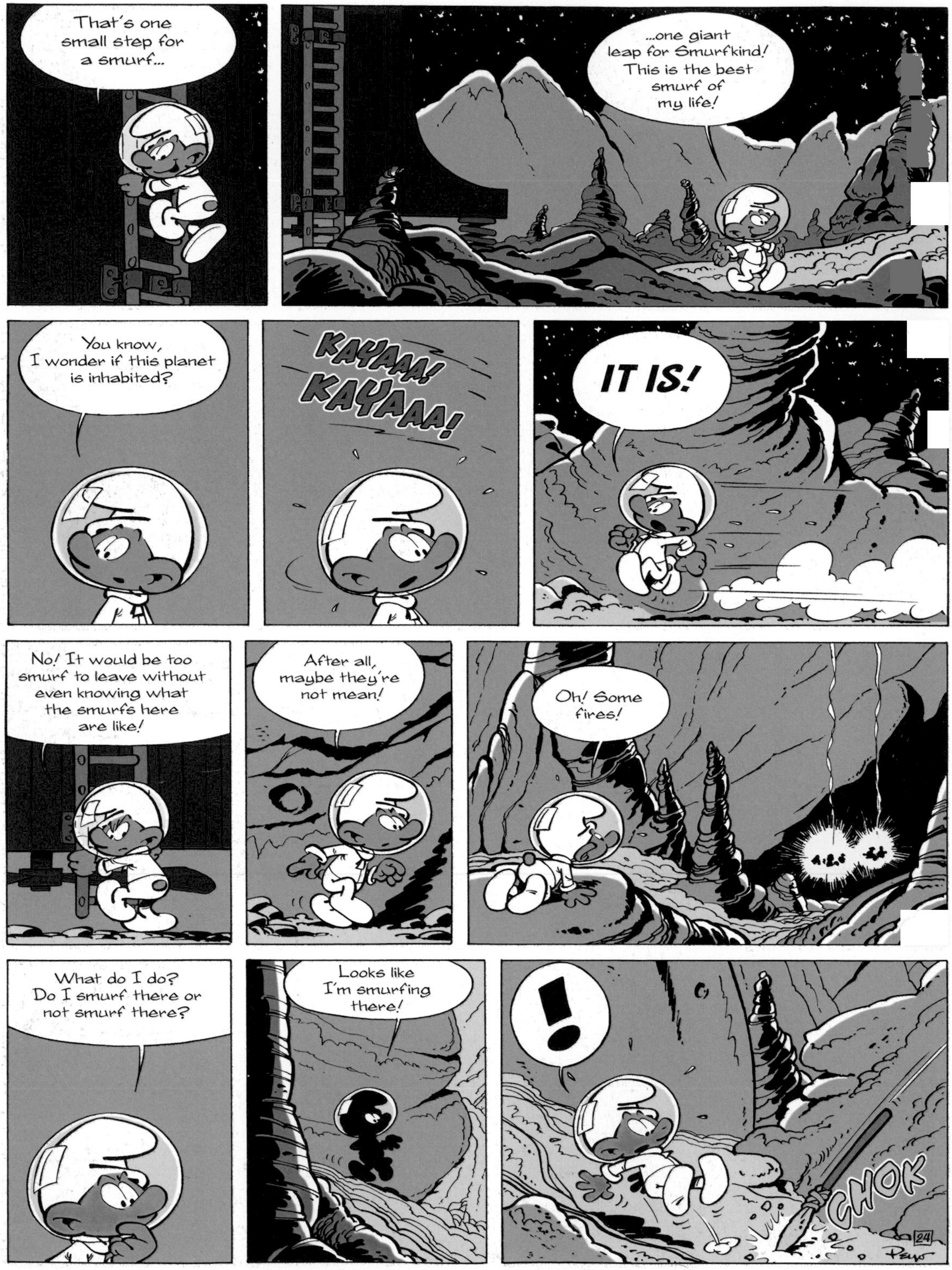
That's one small step for a smurf...
...one giant leap for Smurfkind! This is the best smurf of my life!
You know, I wonder if this planet is inhabited?
KAYAAA! KAYAAA!
IT IS!
No! It would be too smurf to leave without even knowing what the smurfs here are like!
After all, maybe they're not mean!
Oh! Some fires!
What do I do? Do I smurf there or not smurf there?
Looks like I'm smurfing there!
!
CHOK
24
Peyo

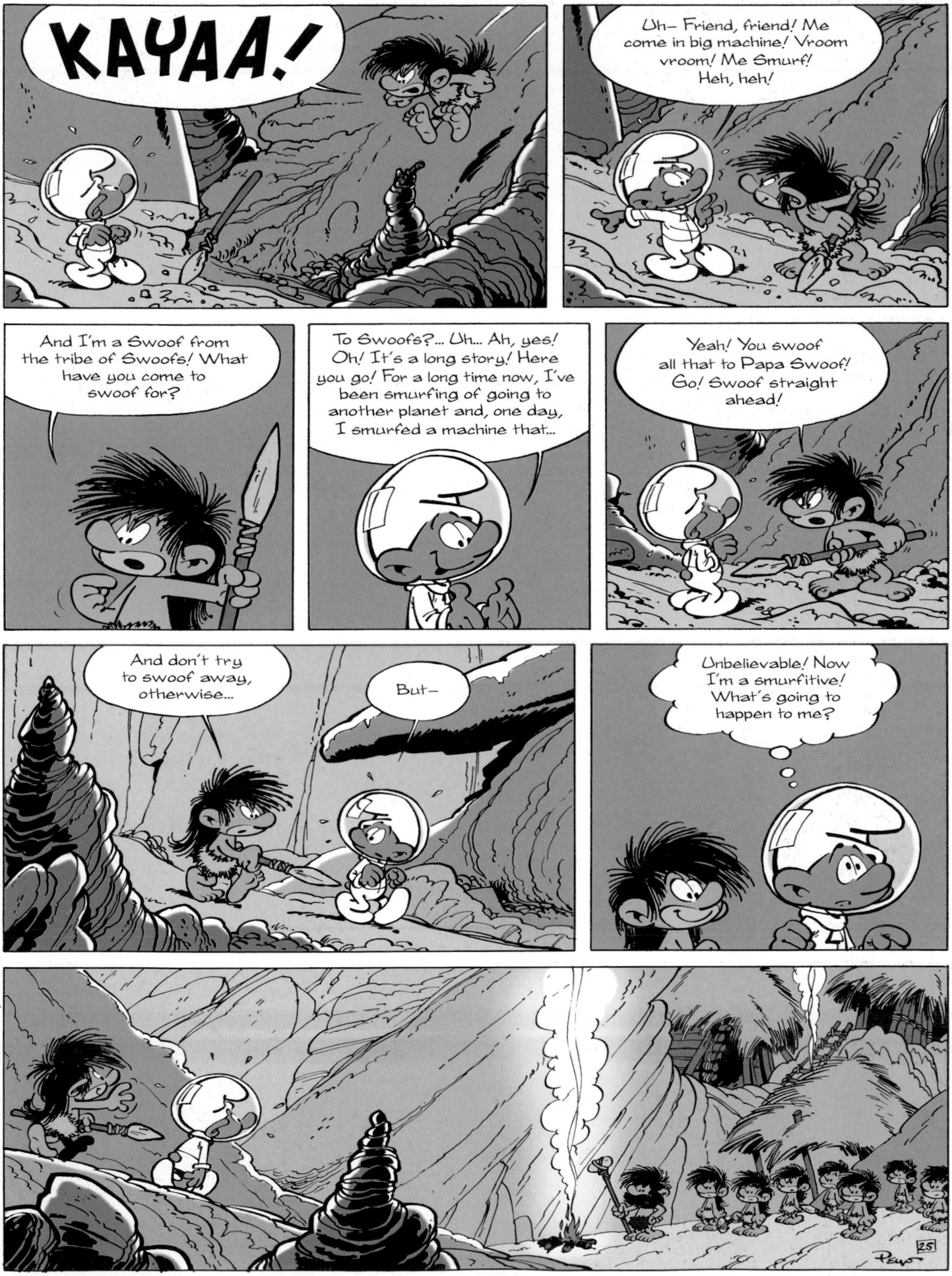

KAYAA!
Uh– Friend, friend! Me come in big machine! Vroom vroom! Me Smurf! Heh, heh!
And I'm a Swoof from the tribe of Swoofs! What have you come to swoof for?
To Swoofs?... Uh... Ah, yes! Oh! It's a long story! Here you go! For a long time now, I've been smurfing of going to another planet and, one day, I smurfed a machine that...
Yeah! You swoof all that to Papa Swoof! Go! Swoof straight ahead!
And don't try to swoof away, otherwise...
But–
Unbelievable! Now I'm a smurfitive! What's going to happen to me?
25

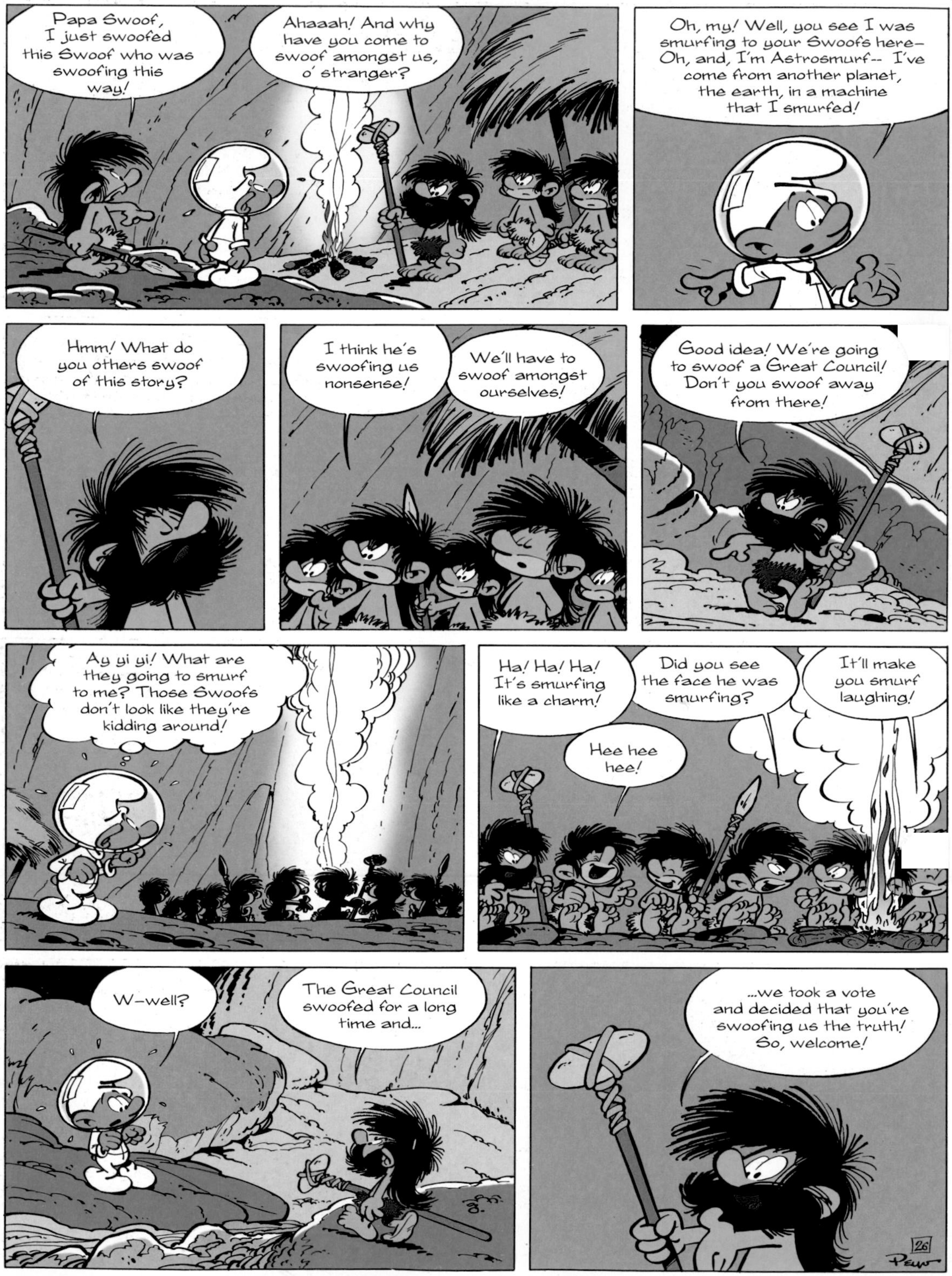
Papa Swoof, I just swoofed this Swoof who was swoofing this way!
Ahaaah! And why have you come to swoof amongst us, o' stranger?
Oh, my! Well, you see I was smurfing to your Swoofs here– Oh, and, I'm Astrosmurf-- I've come from another planet, the earth, in a machine that I smurfed!
Hmm! What do you others swoof of this story?
I think he's swoofing us nonsense!
We'll have to swoof amongst ourselves!
Good idea! We're going to swoof a Great Council! Don't you swoof away from there!
Ay yi yi! What are they going to smurf to me? Those Swoofs don't look like they're kidding around!
Ha! Ha! Ha! It's smurfing like a charm!
Did you see the face he was smurfing?
It'll make you smurf laughing!
Hee hee hee!
W–well?
The Great Council swoofed for a long time and...
...we took a vote and decided that you're swoofing us the truth! So, welcome!
26
Peyo

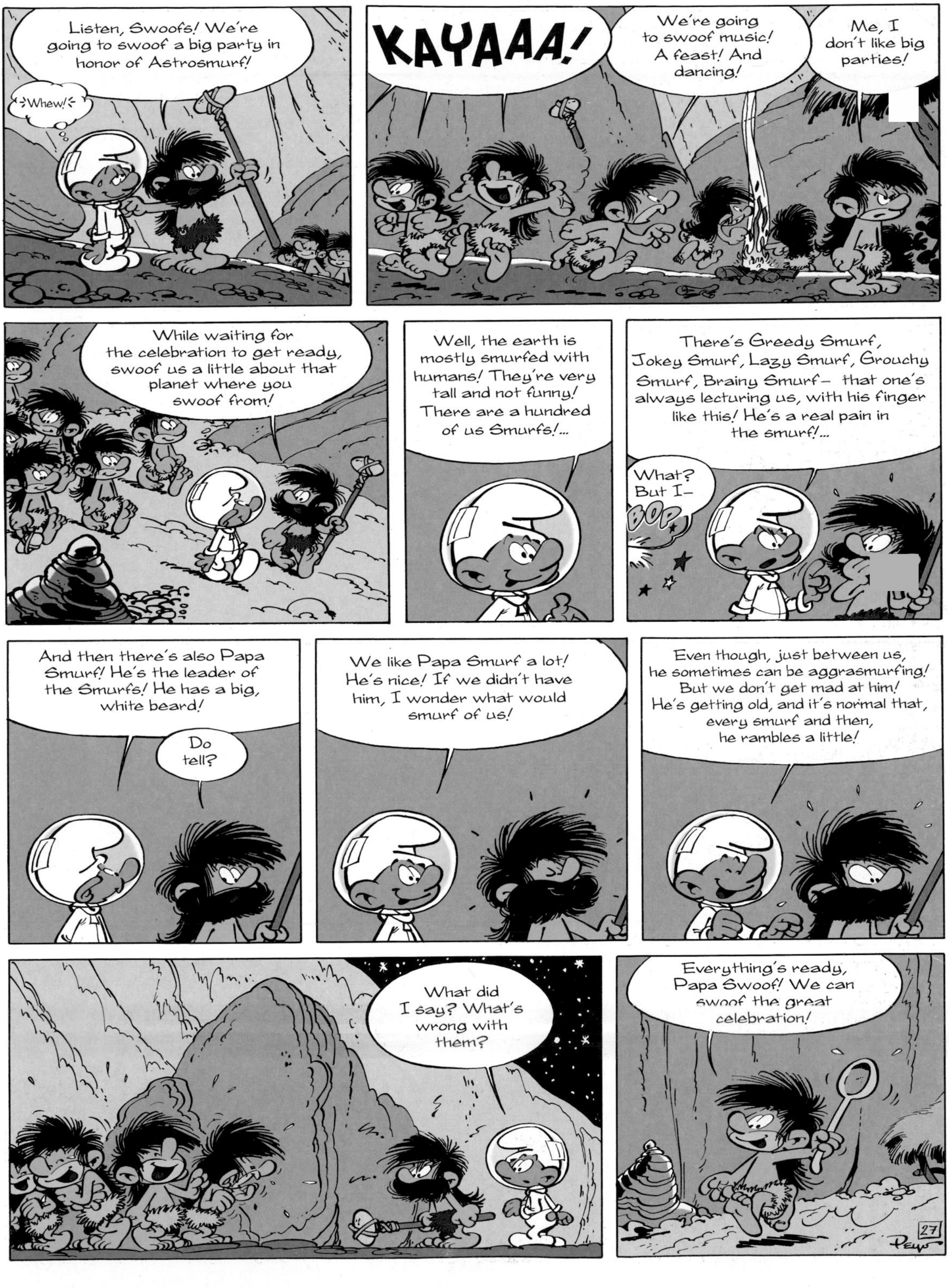
Listen, Swoofs! We're going to swoof a big party in honor of Astrosmurf!
Whew!
KAYAAA!
We're going to swoof music! A feast! And dancing!
Me, I don't like big parties!
While waiting for the celebration to get ready, swoof us a little about that planet where you swoof from!
Well, the earth is mostly smurfed with humans! They're very tall and not funny! There are a hundred of us Smurfs!...
There's Greedy Smurf, Jokey Smurf, Lazy Smurf, Grouchy Smurf, Brainy Smurf– that one's always lecturing us, with his finger like this! He's a real pain in the smurf!...
What? But I–
BOP
And then there's also Papa Smurf! He's the leader of the Smurfs! He has a big, white beard!
Do tell?
We like Papa Smurf a lot! He's nice! If we didn't have him, I wonder what would smurf of us!
Even though, just between us, he sometimes can be aggrasmurfing! But we don't get mad at him! He's getting old, and it's normal that, every smurf and then, he rambles a little!
What did I say? What's wrong with them?
Everything's ready, Papa Swoof! We can swoof the great celebration!
27
Peyo

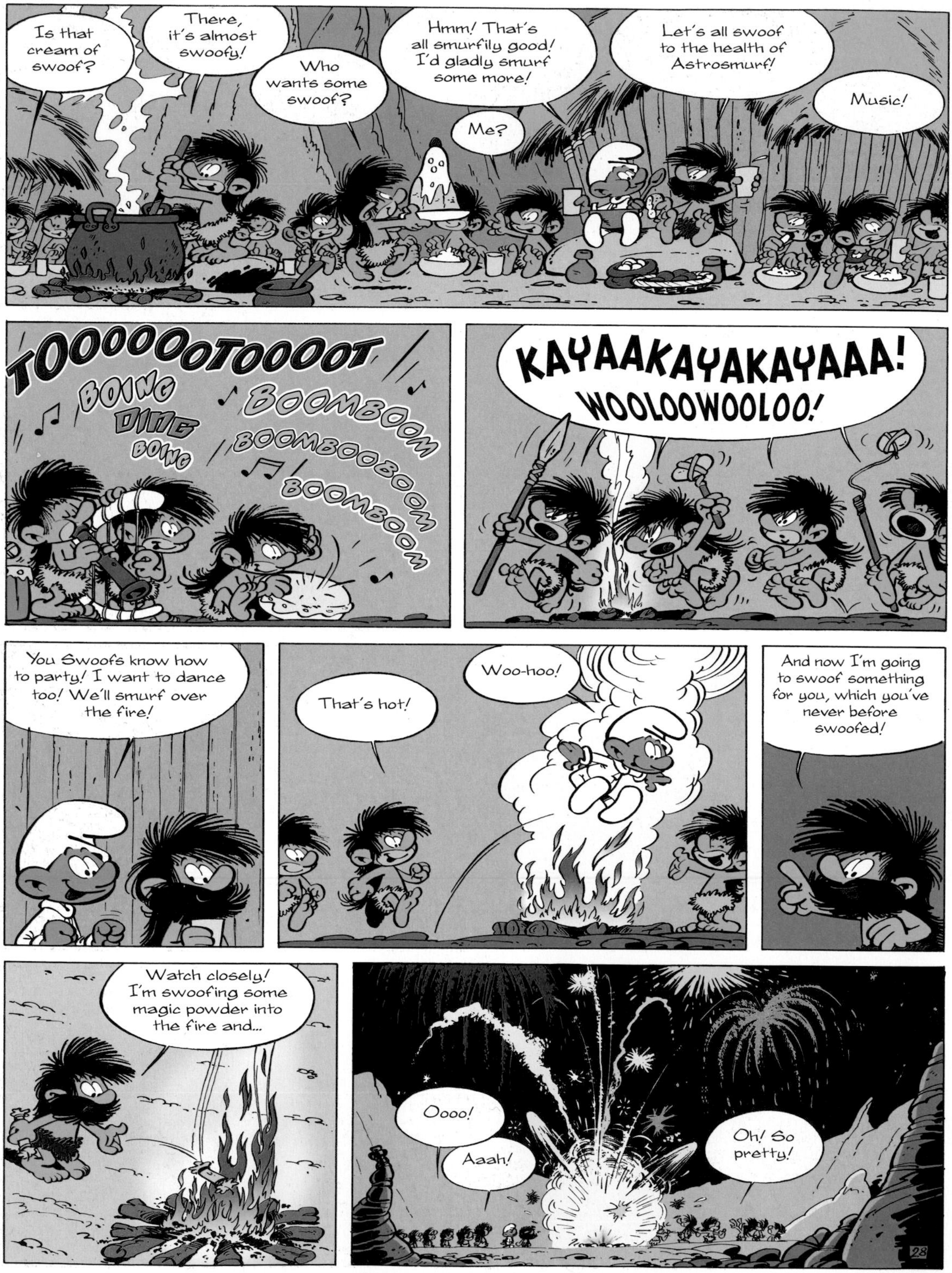
Is that cream of swoof?
There, it's almost swoofy!
Who wants some swoof?
Hmm! That's all smurfily good! I'd gladly smurf some more!
Me?
Let's all swoof to the health of Astrosmurf!
Music!
TOOOOOOTOOOOT
BOING
DING
BOING
BOOMBOOM
BOOMBOOBOOM
BOOMBOOM
KAYAAKAYAKAYAAA!
WOOLOOWOOLOO!
You Swoofs know how to party! I want to dance too! We'll smurf over the fire!
That's hot!
Woo-hoo!
And now I'm going to swoof something for you, which you've never before swoofed!
Watch closely! I'm swoofing some magic powder into the fire and...
Oooo!
Aaah!
Oh! So pretty!
28

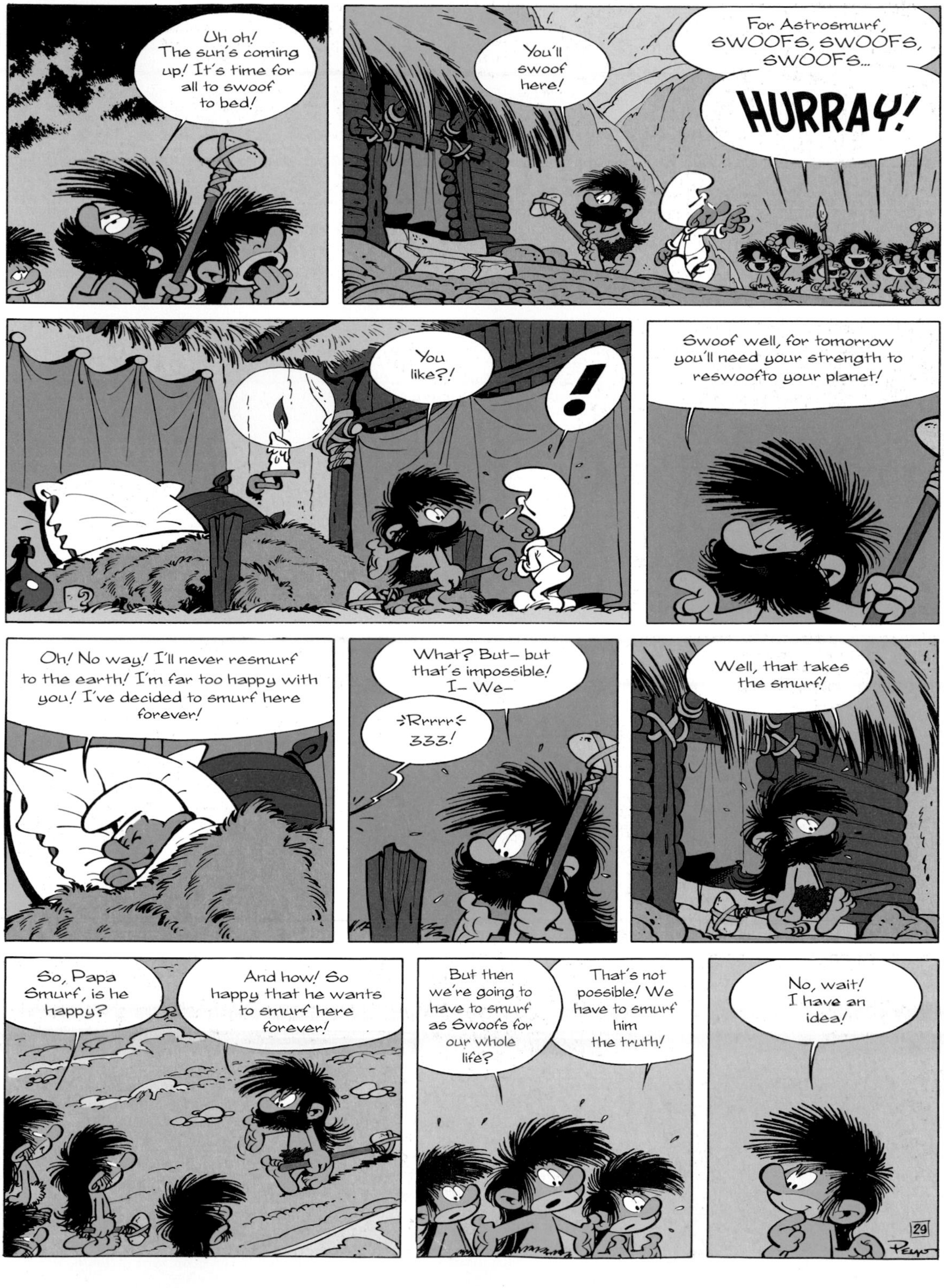
Uh oh! The sun's coming up! It's time for all to swoof to bed!
You'll swoof here!
For Astrosmurf, SWOOFS, SWOOFS, SWOOFS...
HURRAY!
You like?!
!
Swoof well, for tomorrow you'll need your strength to reswoofto your planet!
Oh! No way! I'll never resmurf to the earth! I'm far too happy with you! I've decided to smurf here forever!
What? But– but that's impossible! I– We–
Rrrrr 333!
Well, that takes the smurf!
So, Papa Smurf, is he happy?
And how! So happy that he wants to smurf here forever!
But then we're going to have to smurf as Swoofs for our whole life?
That's not possible! We have to smurf him the truth!
No, wait! I have an idea!
29

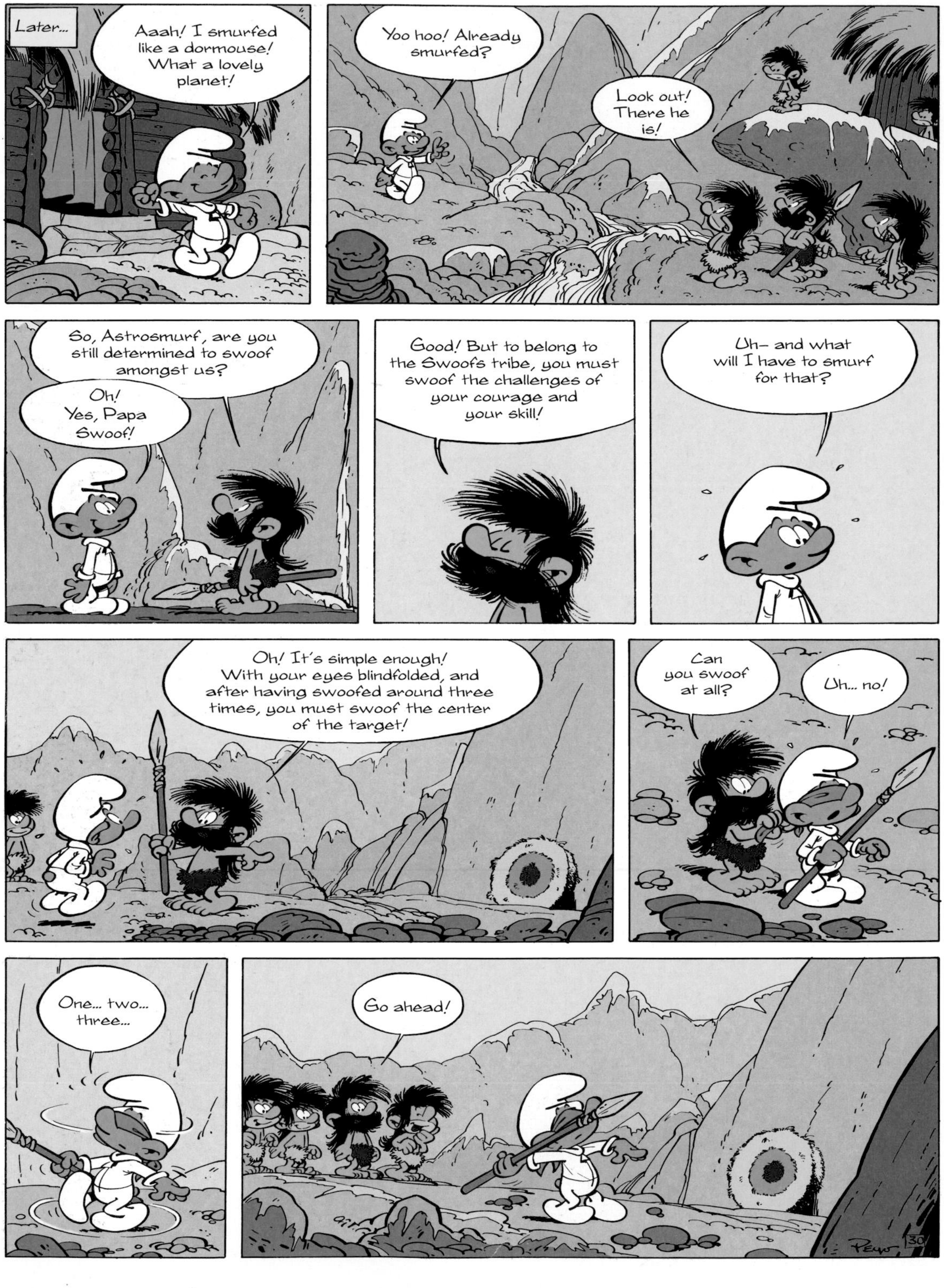
Later...
Aaah! I smurfed like a dormouse! What a lovely planet!
Yoo hoo! Already smurfed?
Look out! There he is!
So, Astrosmurf, are you still determined to swoof amongst us?
Oh! Yes, Papa Swoof!
Good! But to belong to the Swoofs tribe, you must swoof the challenges of your courage and your skill!
Uh– and what will I have to smurf for that?
Oh! It's simple enough! With your eyes blindfolded, and after having swoofed around three times, you must swoof the center of the target!
Can you swoof at all?
Uh... no!
One... two... three...
Go ahead!
30

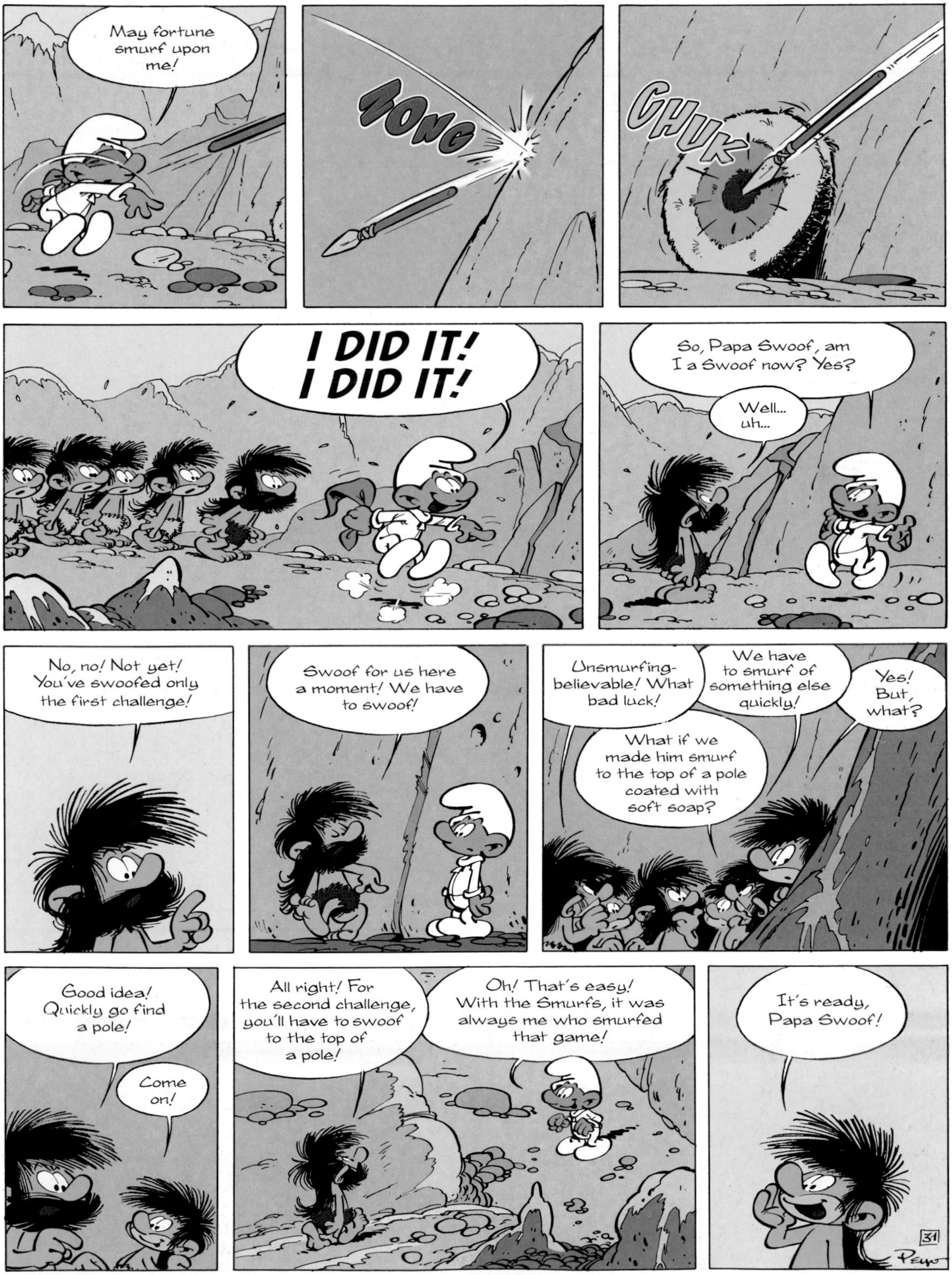
May fortune smurf upon me!
BONG
CHUK
I DID IT! I DID IT!
So, Papa Swoof, am I a Swoof now? Yes?
Well... uh...
No, no! Not yet! You've swoofed only the first challenge!
Swoof for us here a moment! We have to swoof!
Unsmurfing-believable! What bad luck!
We have to smurf of something else quickly!
Yes! But, what?
What if we made him smurf to the top of a pole coated with soft soap?
Good idea! Quickly go find a pole!
Come on!
All right! For the second challenge, you'll have to swoof to the top of a pole!
Oh! That's easy! With the Smurfs, it was always me who smurfed that game!
It's ready, Papa Swoof!
31
Peyo

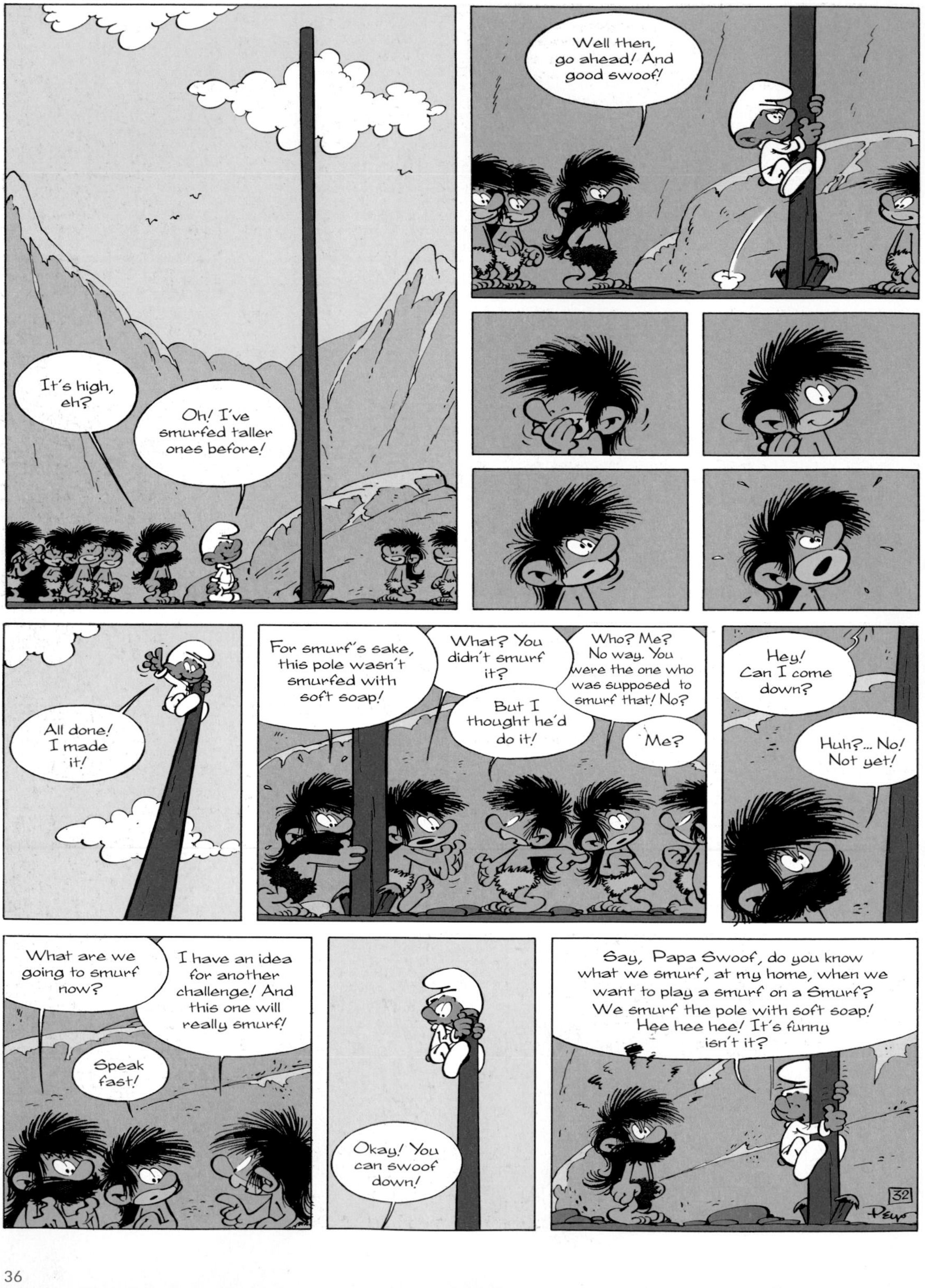
It's high, eh?
Oh! I've smurfed taller ones before!
Well then, go ahead! And good swoof!
All done! I made it!
For smurf's sake, this pole wasn't smurfed with soft soap!
What? You didn't smurf it?
Who? Me? No way. You were the one who was supposed to smurf that! No?
But I thought he'd do it!
Me?
Hey! Can I come down?
Huh?... No! Not yet!
What are we going to smurf now?
I have an idea for another challenge! And this one will really smurf!
Speak fast!
Okay! You can swoof down!
Say, Papa Swoof, do you know what we smurf, at my home, when we want to play a smurf on a Smurf? We smurf the pole with soft soap! Hee hee hee! It's funny isn't it?
32
Peyo

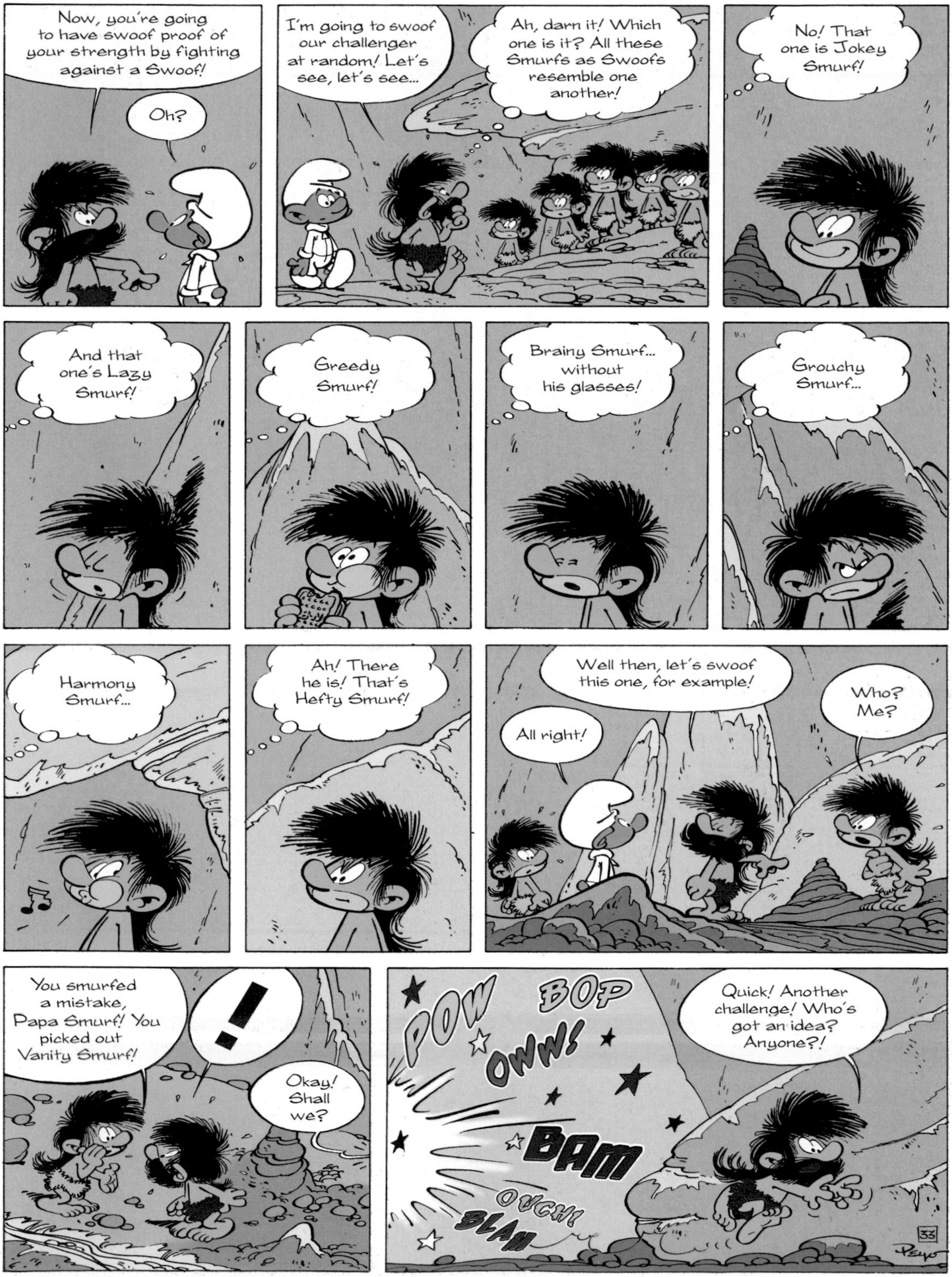
Now, you're going to have swoof proof of your strength by fighting against a Swoof!
Oh?
I'm going to swoof our challenger at random! Let's see, let's see...
Ah, darn it! Which one is it? All these Smurfs as Swoofs resemble one another!
No! That one is Jokey Smurf!
And that one's Lazy Smurf!
Greedy Smurf!
Brainy Smurf... without his glasses!
Grouchy Smurf...
Harmony Smurf...
Ah! There he is! That's Hefty Smurf!
Well then, let's swoof this one, for example!
All right!
Who? Me?
You smurfed a mistake, Papa Smurf! You picked out Vanity Smurf!
!
Okay! Shall we?
POW
BOP
OWW!
BAM
OUCH!
BLAM
Quick! Another challenge! Who's got an idea? Anyone?!
33
PEYO

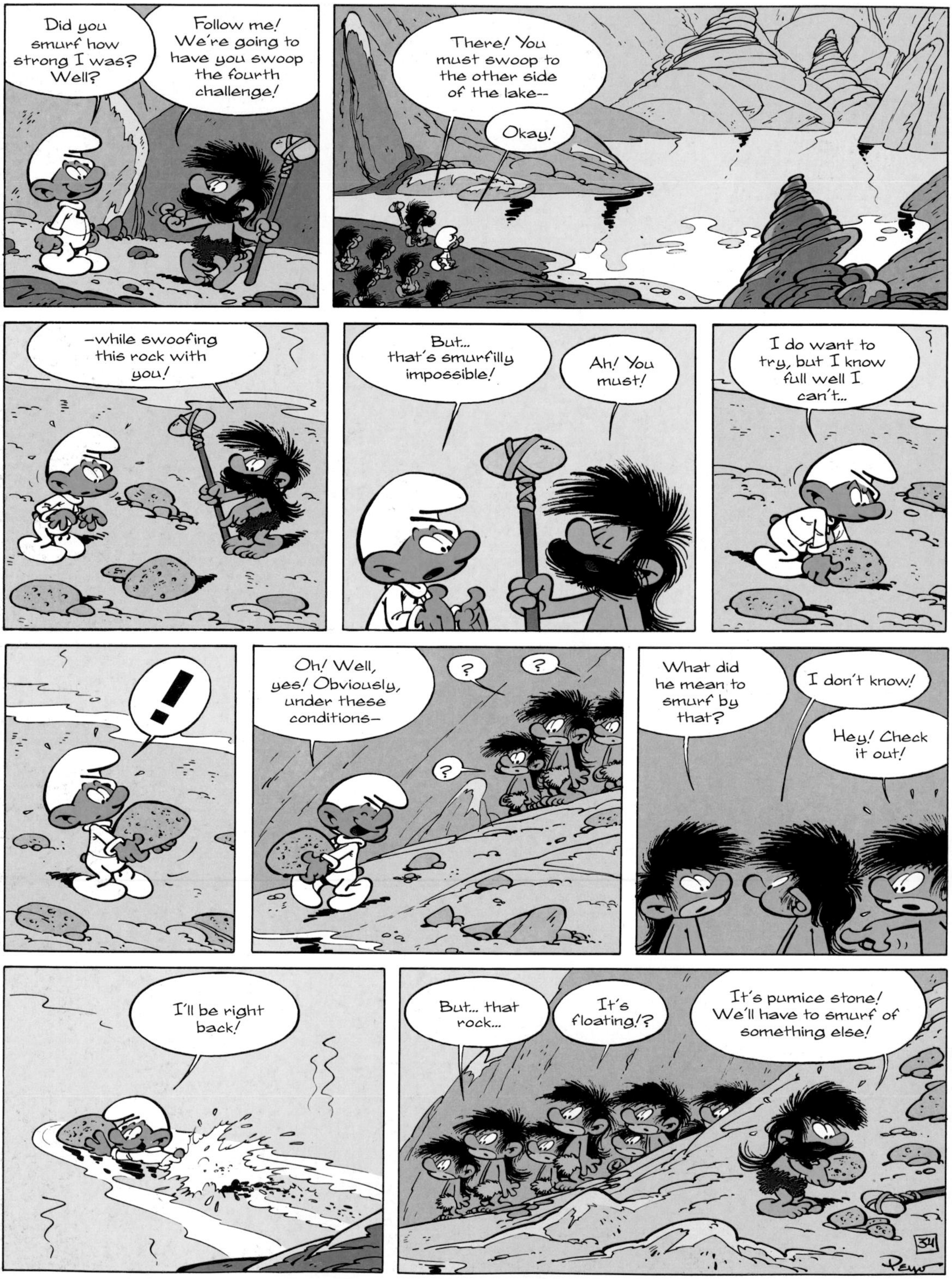

Did you smurf how strong I was? Well?
Follow me! We're going to have you swoop the fourth challenge!
There! You must swoop to the other side of the lake--
Okay!
-while swoofing this rock with you!
But... that's smurfilly impossible!
Ah! You must!
I do want to try, but I know full well I can't...
!
Oh! Well, yes! Obviously, under these conditions-
?
?
?
What did he mean to smurf by that?
I don't know!
Hey! Check it out!
I'll be right back!
But... that rock...
It's floating!?
It's pumice stone! We'll have to smurf of something else!
34

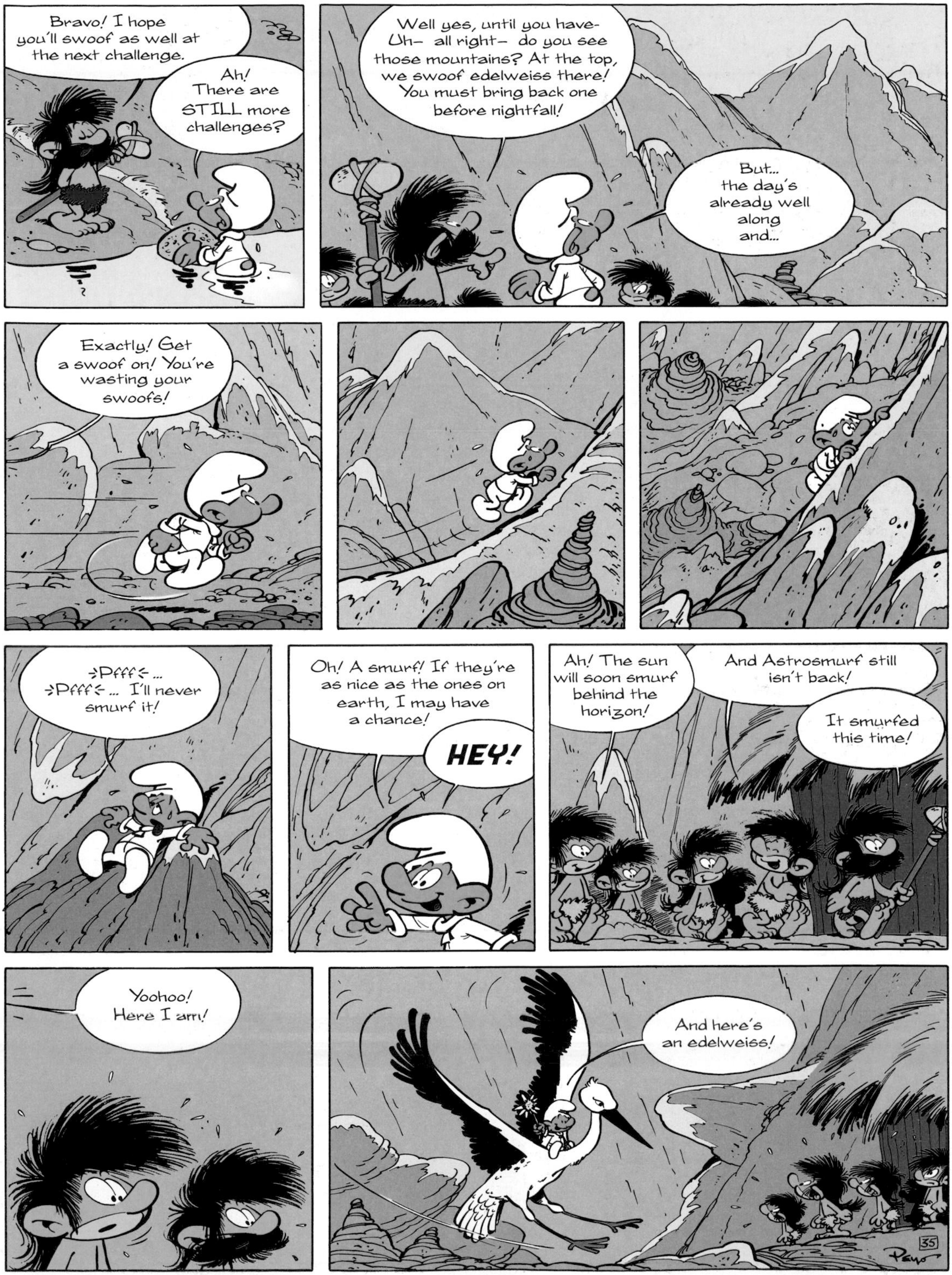
Bravo! I hope you'll swoof as well at the next challenge.
Ah! There are STILL more challenges?
Well yes, until you have- Uh- all right- do you see those mountains? At the top, we swoof edelweiss there! You must bring back one before nightfall!
But... the day's already well along and...
Exactly! Get a swoof on! You're wasting your swoofs!
»Pfff«... »Pfff«... I'll never smurf it!
Oh! A smurf! If they're as nice as the ones on earth, I may have a chance!
HEY!
Ah! The sun will soon smurf behind the horizon!
And Astrosmurf still isn't back!
It smurfed this time!
Yoohoo! Here I am!
And here's an edelweiss!
35
Peyo

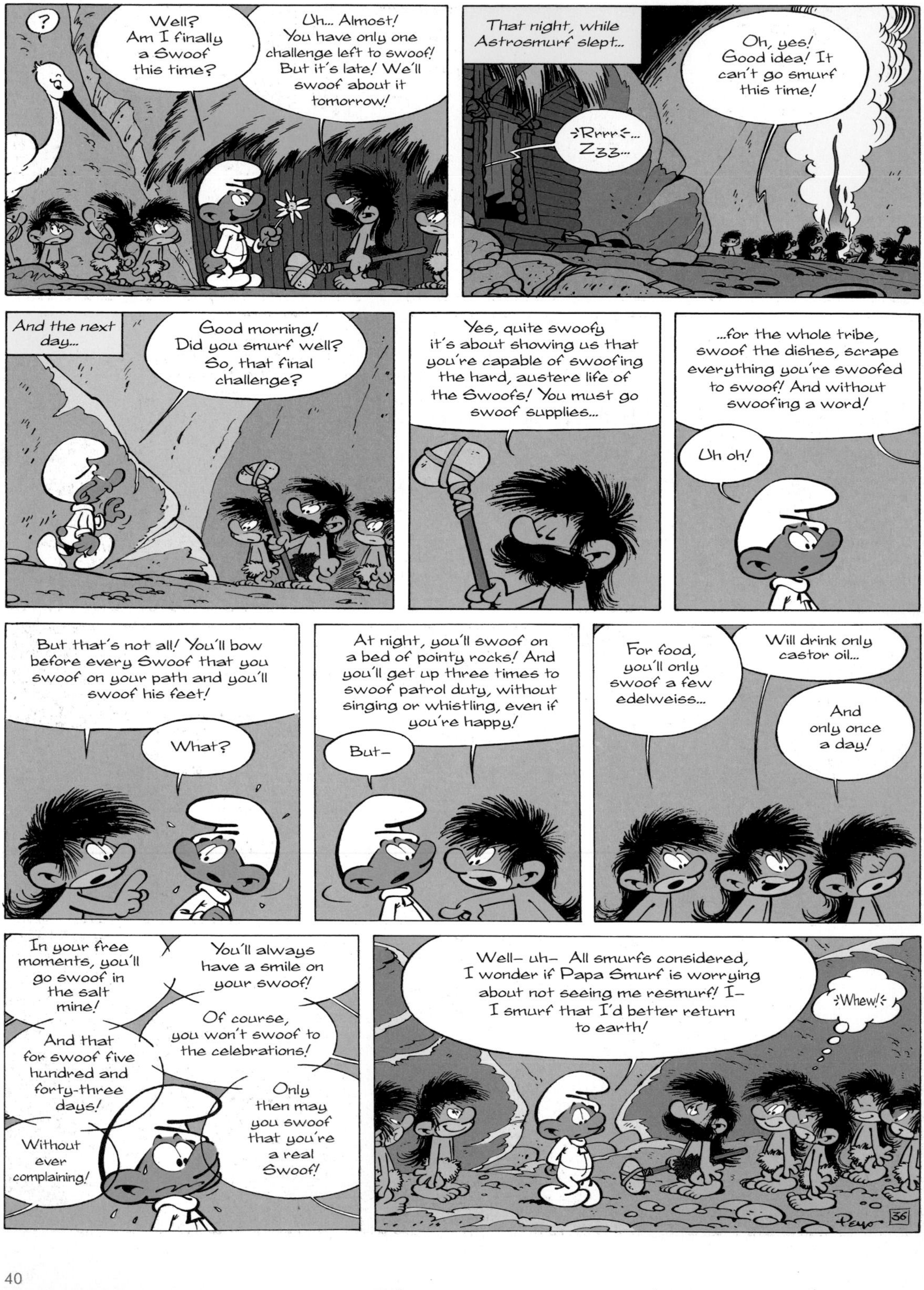
?
Well? Am I finally a Swoof this time?
Uh... Almost! You have only one challenge left to swoof! But it's late! We'll swoof about it tomorrow!
That night, while Astrosmurf slept...
Rrrr... Zzz...
Oh, yes! Good idea! It can't go smurf this time!
And the next day...
Good morning! Did you smurf well? So, that final challenge?
Yes, quite swoofy it's about showing us that you're capable of swoofing the hard, austere life of the Swoofs! You must go swoof supplies...
...for the whole tribe, swoof the dishes, scrape everything you're swoofed to swoof! And without swoofing a word!
Uh oh!
But that's not all! You'll bow before every Swoof that you swoof on your path and you'll swoof his feet!
What?
At night, you'll swoof on a bed of pointy rocks! And you'll get up three times to swoof patrol duty, without singing or whistling, even if you're happy!
But–
For food, you'll only swoof a few edelweiss...
Will drink only castor oil...
And only once a day!
In your free moments, you'll go swoof in the salt mine!
You'll always have a smile on your swoof!
Of course, you won't swoof to the celebrations!
And that for swoof five hundred and forty-three days!
Only then may you swoof that you're a real Swoof!
Without ever complaining!
Well– uh– All smurfs considered, I wonder if Papa Smurf is worrying about not seeing me resmurf! I– I smurf that I'd better return to earth!
Whew!
Peyo
36

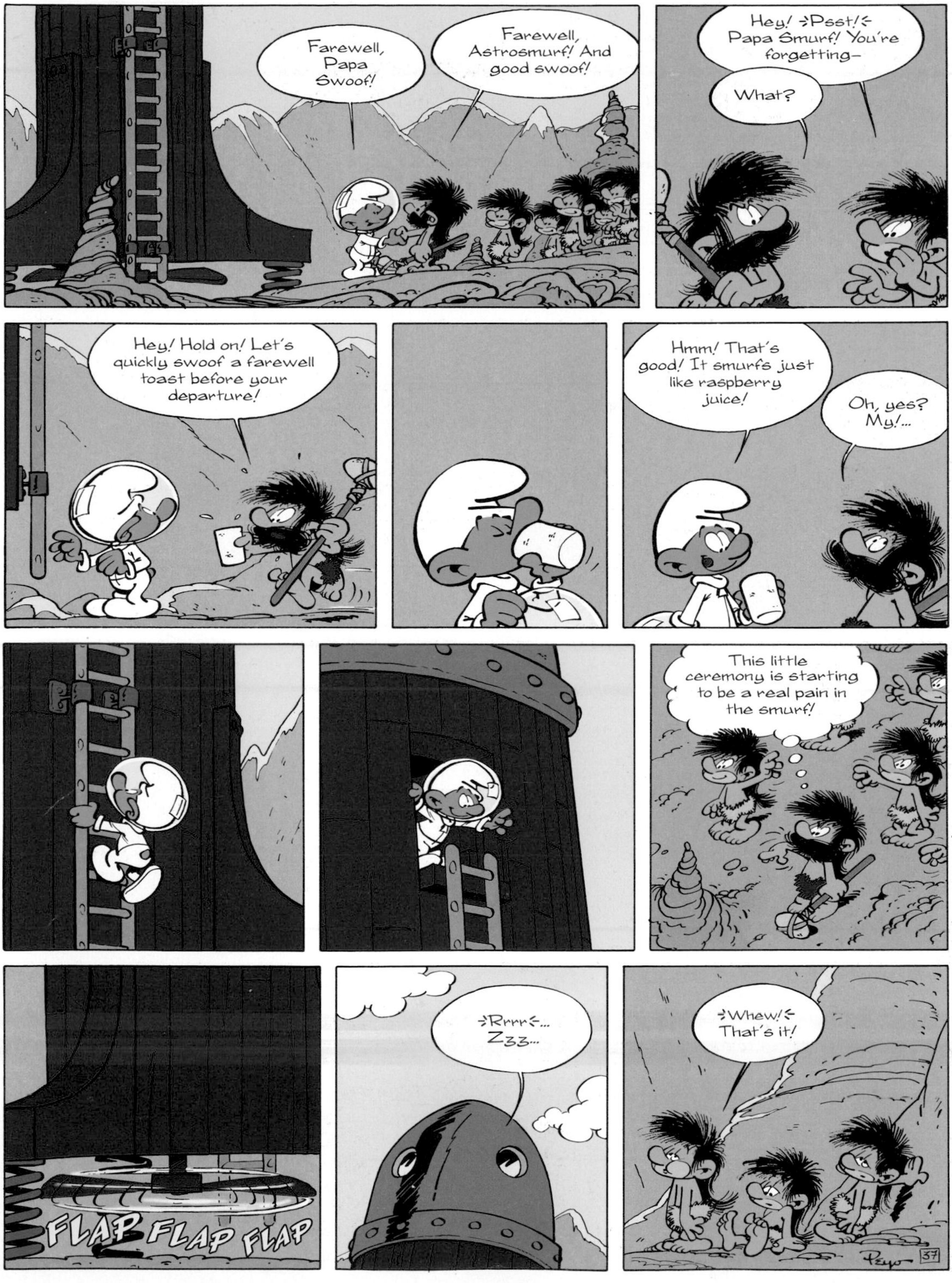
Farewell, Papa Swoof!
Farewell, Astrosmurf! And good swoof!
Hey! Psst! Papa Smurf! You're forgetting–
What?
Hey! Hold on! Let's quickly swoof a farewell toast before your departure!
Hmm! That's good! It smurfs just like raspberry juice!
Oh, yes? My!...
This little ceremony is starting to be a real pain in the smurf!
FLAP FLAP FLAP
Rrrr... Zzz...
Whew! That's it!
37

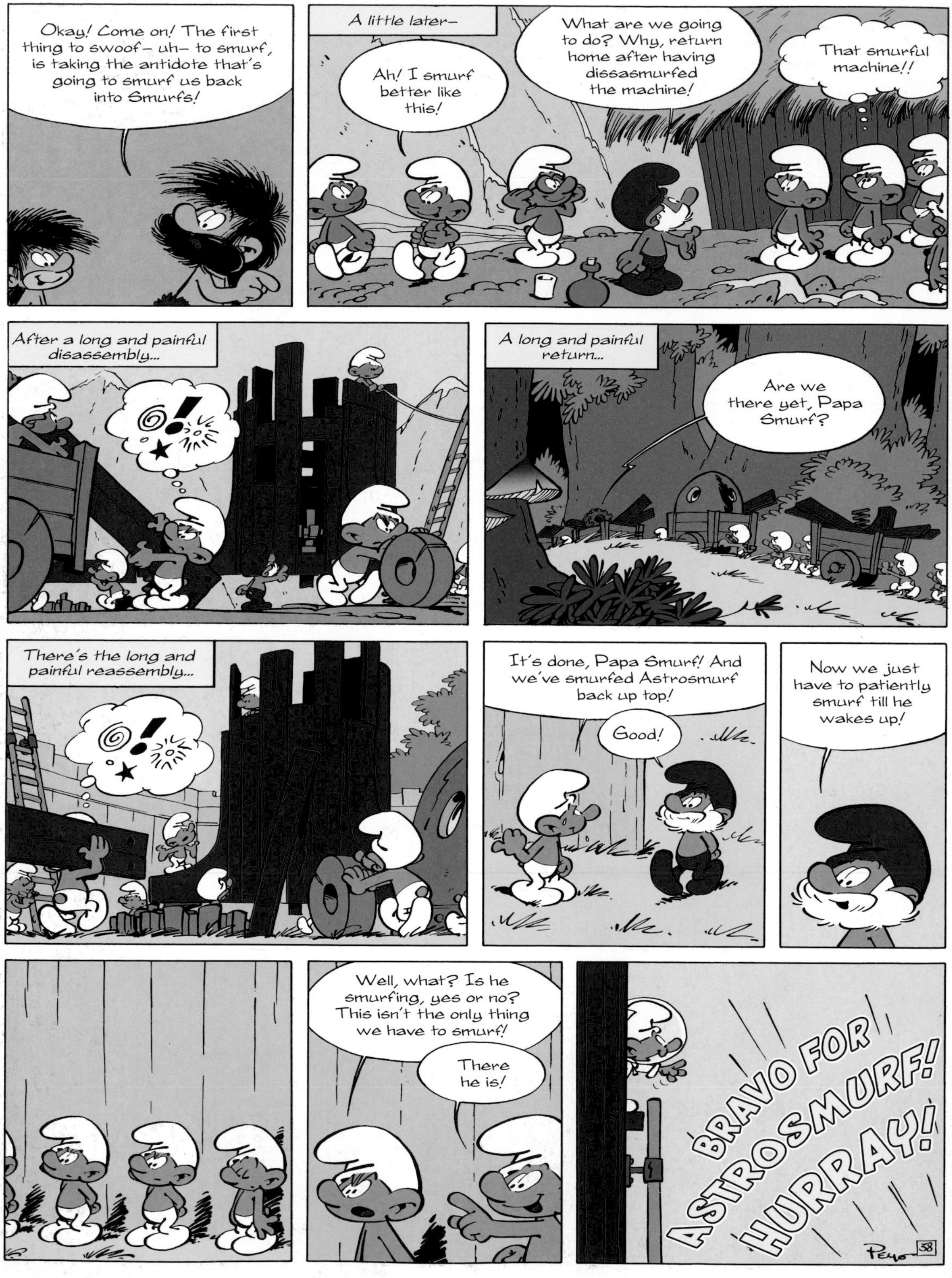
Okay! Come on! The first thing to swoof– uh– to smurf, is taking the antidote that's going to smurf us back into Smurfs!
A little later–
Ah! I smurf better like this!
What are we going to do? Why, return home after having dissasmurfed the machine!
That smurful machine!!
After a long and painful disassembly...
A long and painful return...
Are we there yet, Papa Smurf?
There's the long and painful reassembly...
It's done, Papa Smurf! And we've smurfed Astrosmurf back up top!
Good!
Now we just have to patiently smurf till he wakes up!
Well, what? Is he smurfing, yes or no? This isn't the only thing we have to smurf!
There he is!
BRAVO FOR ASTROSMURF! HURRAY!
Peyo
38

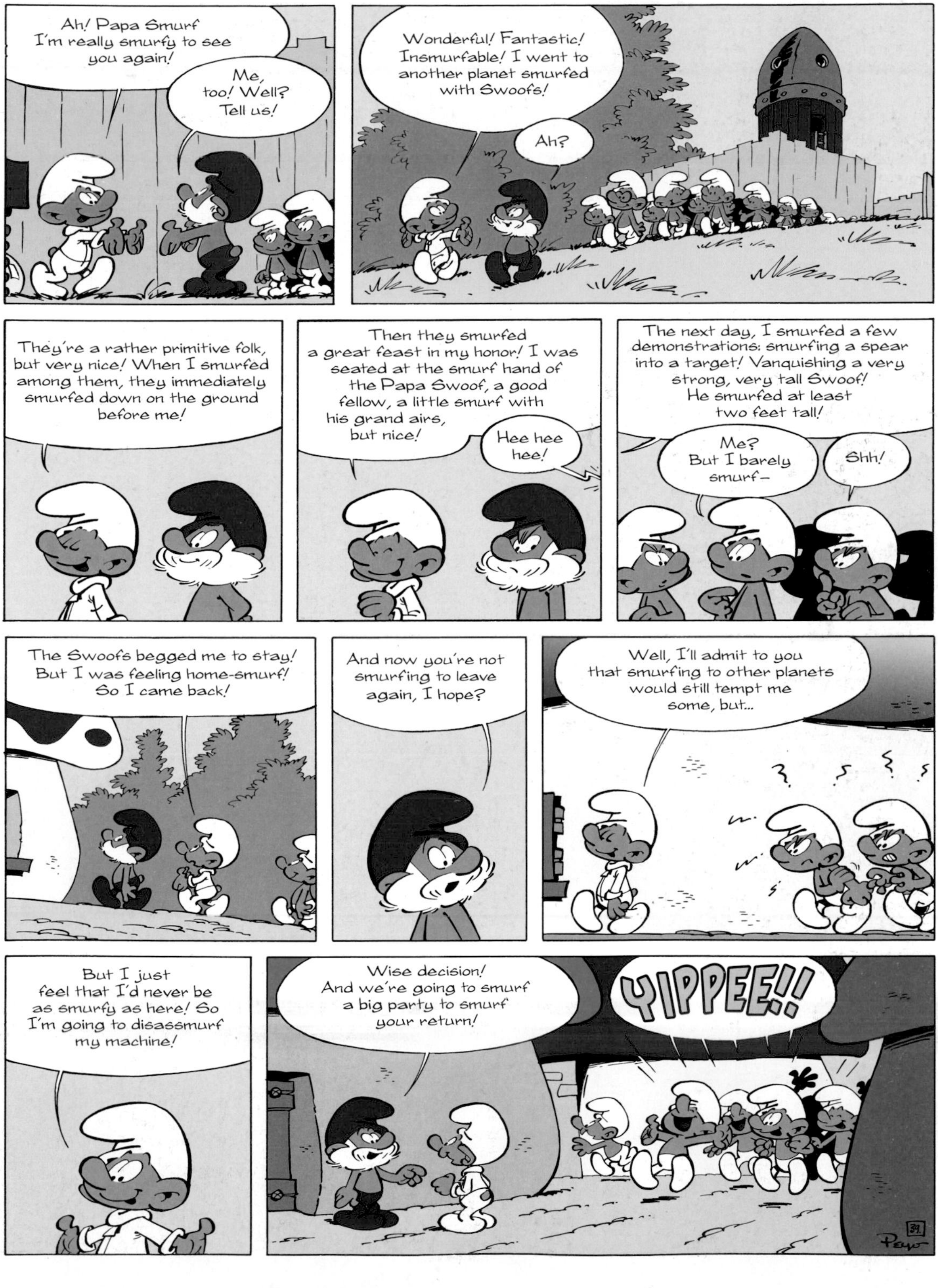

Ah! Papa Smurf I'm really smurfy to see you again!
Me, too! Well? Tell us!
Wonderful! Fantastic! Insmurfable! I went to another planet smurfed with Swoofs!
Ah?
They're a rather primitive folk, but very nice! When I smurfed among them, they immediately smurfed down on the ground before me!
Then they smurfed a great feast in my honor! I was seated at the smurf hand of the Papa Swoof, a good fellow, a little smurf with his grand airs, but nice!
Hee hee hee!
The next day, I smurfed a few demonstrations: smurfing a spear into a target! Vanquishing a very strong, very tall Swoof! He smurfed at least two feet tall!
Me? But I barely smurf–
Shh!
The Swoofs begged me to stay! But I was feeling home-smurf! So I came back!
And now you're not smurfing to leave again, I hope?
Well, I'll admit to you that smurfing to other planets would still tempt me some, but...
But I just feel that I'd never be as smurfy as here! So I'm going to disassmurf my machine!
Wise decision! And we're going to smurf a big party to smurf your return!
YIPPEE!!

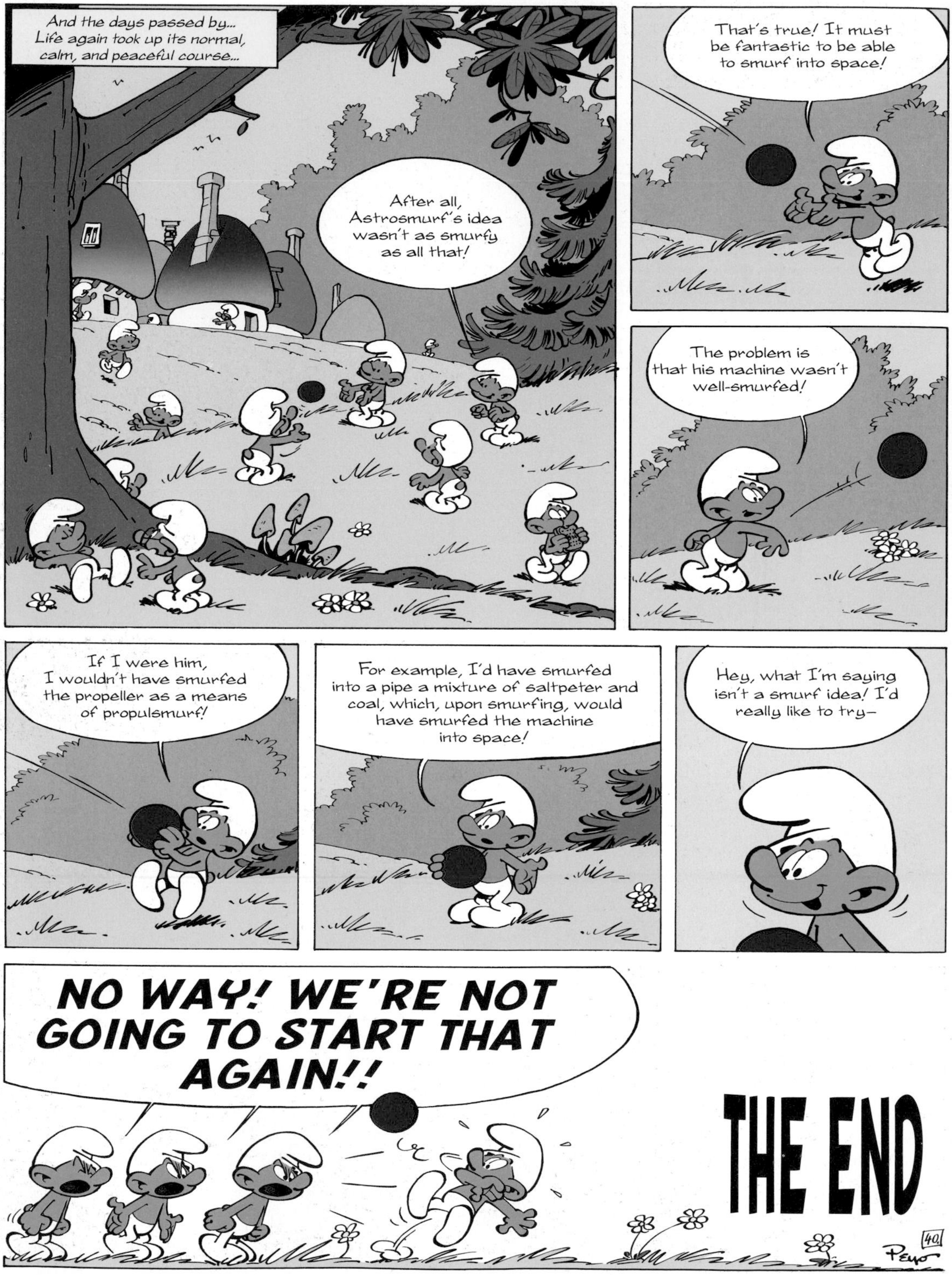
And the days passed by... Life again took up its normal, calm, and peaceful course...
After all, Astrosmurf's idea wasn't as smurfy as all that!
That's true! It must be fantastic to be able to smurf into space!
The problem is that his machine wasn't well-smurfed!
If I were him, I wouldn't have smurfed the propeller as a means of propulsmurf!
For example, I'd have smurfed into a pipe a mixture of saltpeter and coal, which, upon smurfing, would have smurfed the machine into space!
Hey, what I'm saying isn't a smurf idea! I'd really like to try–
NO WAY! WE'RE NOT GOING TO START THAT AGAIN!!
THE END
40
Peyo

THE SMURF SUBMARINE

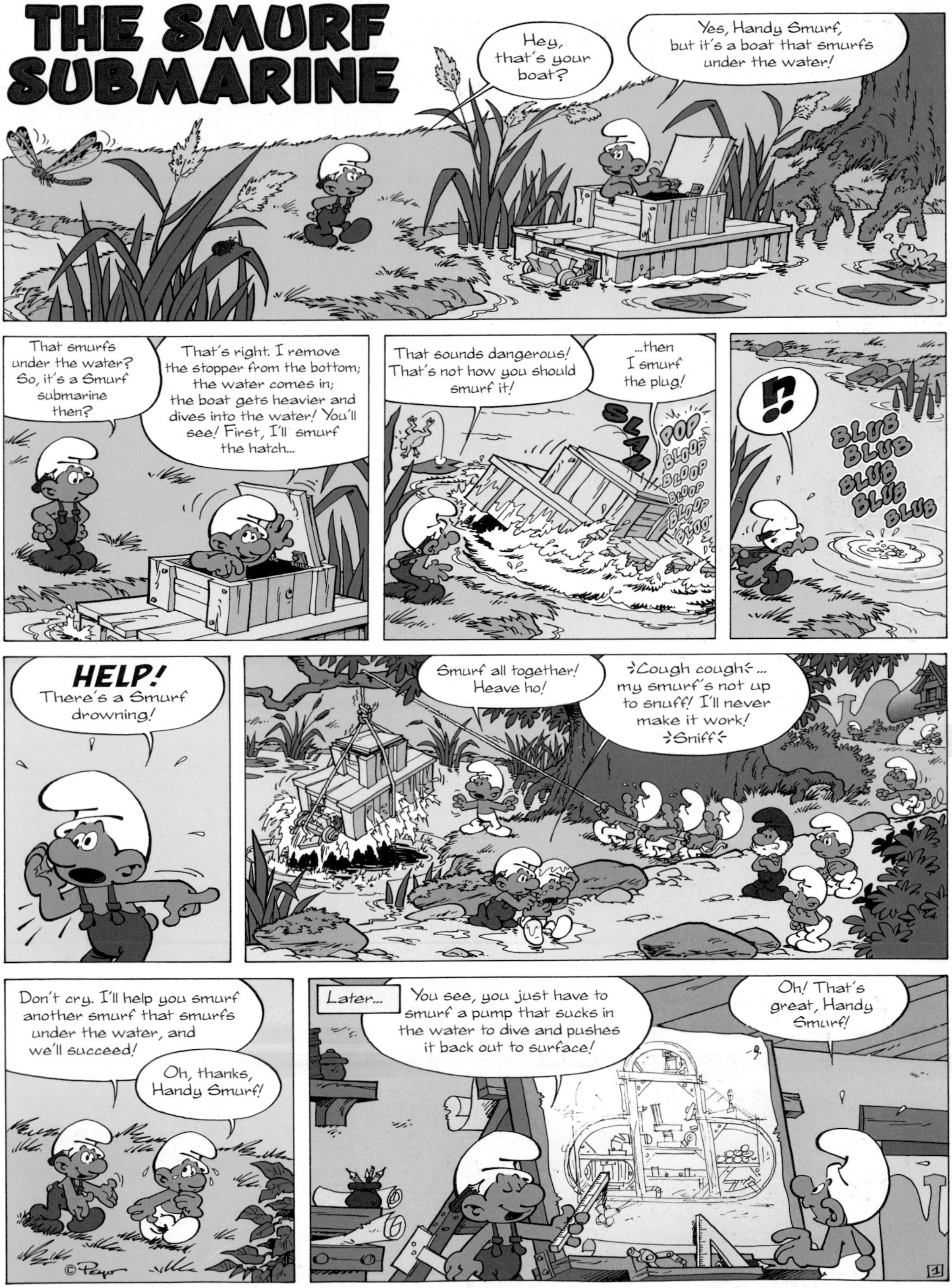

Hey, that's your boat?
Yes, Handy Smurf, but it's a boat that smurfs under the water!
That smurfs under the water? So, it's a Smurf submarine then?
That's right. I remove the stopper from the bottom; the water comes in; the boat gets heavier and dives into the water! You'll see! First, I'll smurf the hatch...
That sounds dangerous! That's not how you should smurf it!
...then I smurf the plug!
SLAM
POP
BLOOP BLOOP BLOOP BLOOP BLOO
?!
BLUB BLUB BLUB BLUB BLUB
HELP! There's a Smurf drowning!
Smurf all together! Heave ho!
Cough cough ... my smurf's not up to snuff! I'll never make it work! Sniff
Don't cry. I'll help you smurf another smurf that smurfs under the water, and we'll succeed!
Oh, thanks, Handy Smurf!
© Peyo
Later...
You see, you just have to smurf a pump that sucks in the water to dive and pushes it back out to surface!
Oh! That's great, Handy Smurf!
1

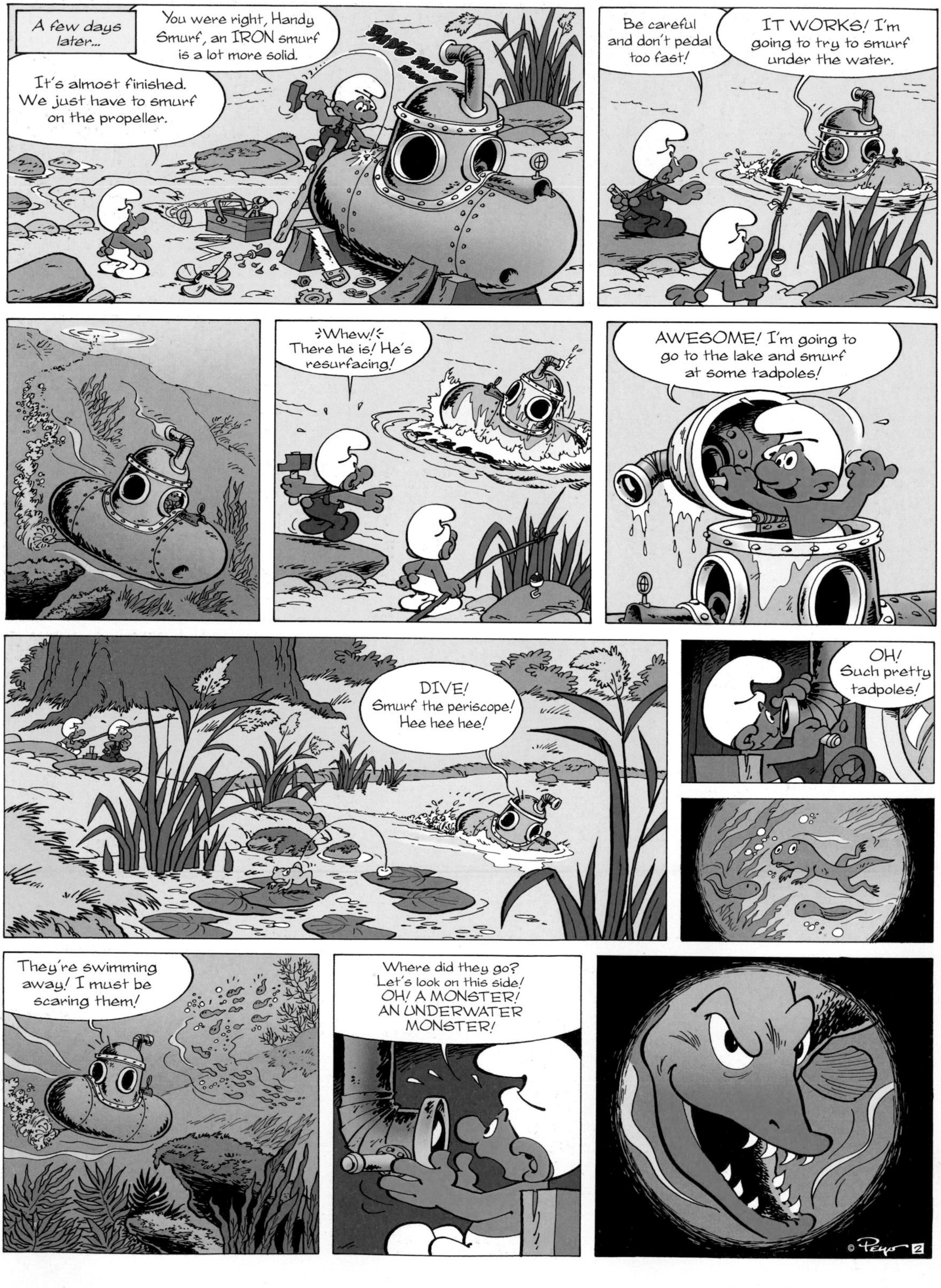
A few days later...
You were right, Handy Smurf, an IRON smurf is a lot more solid.
It's almost finished. We just have to smurf on the propeller.
Be careful and don't pedal too fast!
IT WORKS! I'm going to try to smurf under the water.
Whew! There he is! He's resurfacing!
AWESOME! I'm going to go to the lake and smurf at some tadpoles!
DIVE! Smurf the periscope! Hee hee hee!
OH! Such pretty tadpoles!
They're swimming away! I must be scaring them!
Where did they go? Let's look on this side! OH! A MONSTER! AN UNDERWATER MONSTER!
© Peyo 2

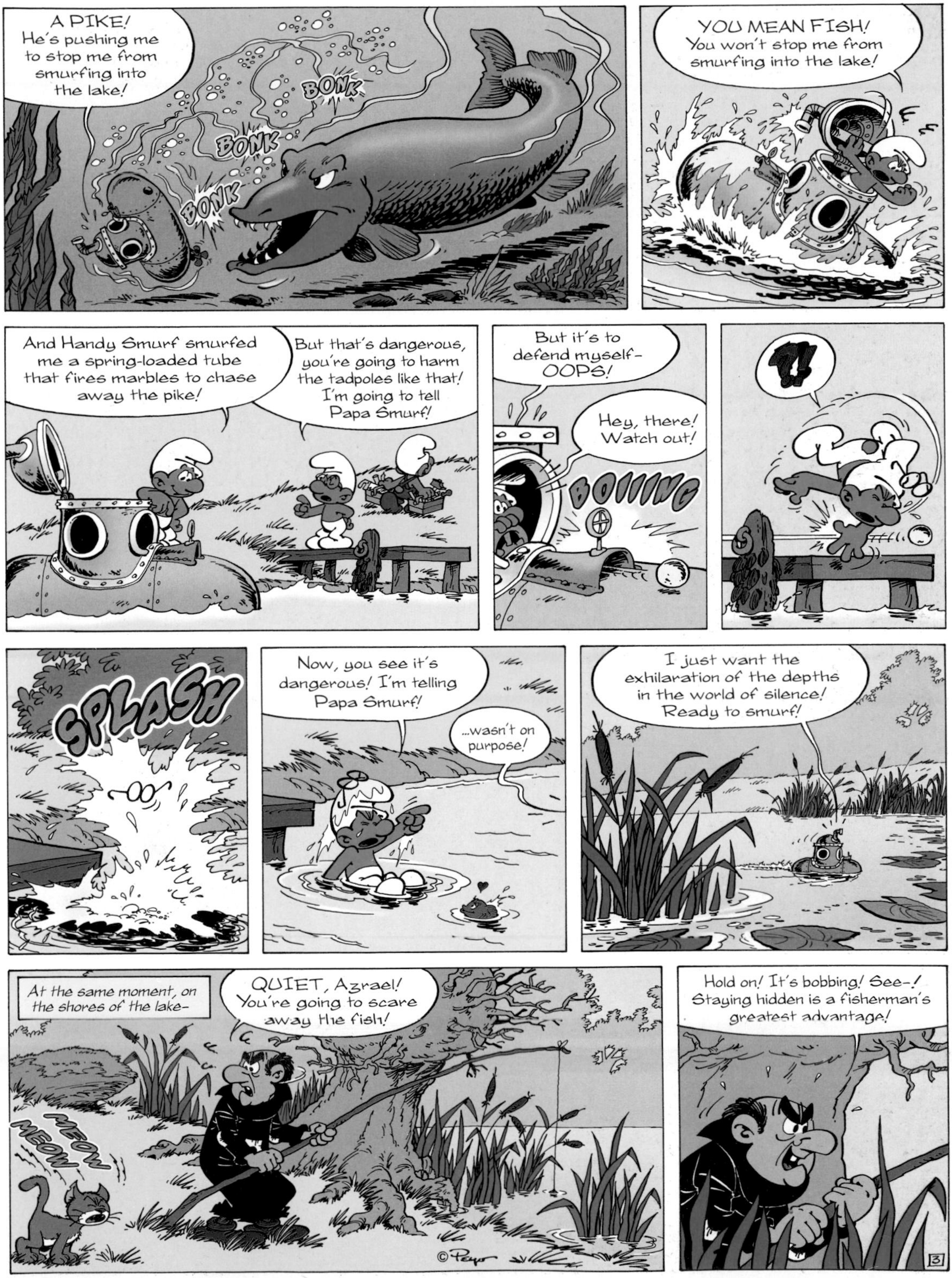
A PIKE! He's pushing me to stop me from smurfing into the lake!
BONK
BONK
BONK
YOU MEAN FISH! You won't stop me from smurfing into the lake!
And Handy Smurf smurfed me a spring-loaded tube that fires marbles to chase away the pike!
But that's dangerous, you're going to harm the tadpoles like that! I'm going to tell Papa Smurf!
But it's to defend myself— OOPS!
Hey, there! Watch out!
BOIIING
SPLASH
Now, you see it's dangerous! I'm telling Papa Smurf!
...wasn't on purpose!
I just want the exhilaration of the depths in the world of silence! Ready to smurf!
At the same moment, on the shores of the lake—
QUIET, Azrael! You're going to scare away the fish!
MEOW
MEOW
© Peyo
Hold on! It's bobbing! See—! Staying hidden is a fisherman's greatest advantage!
3

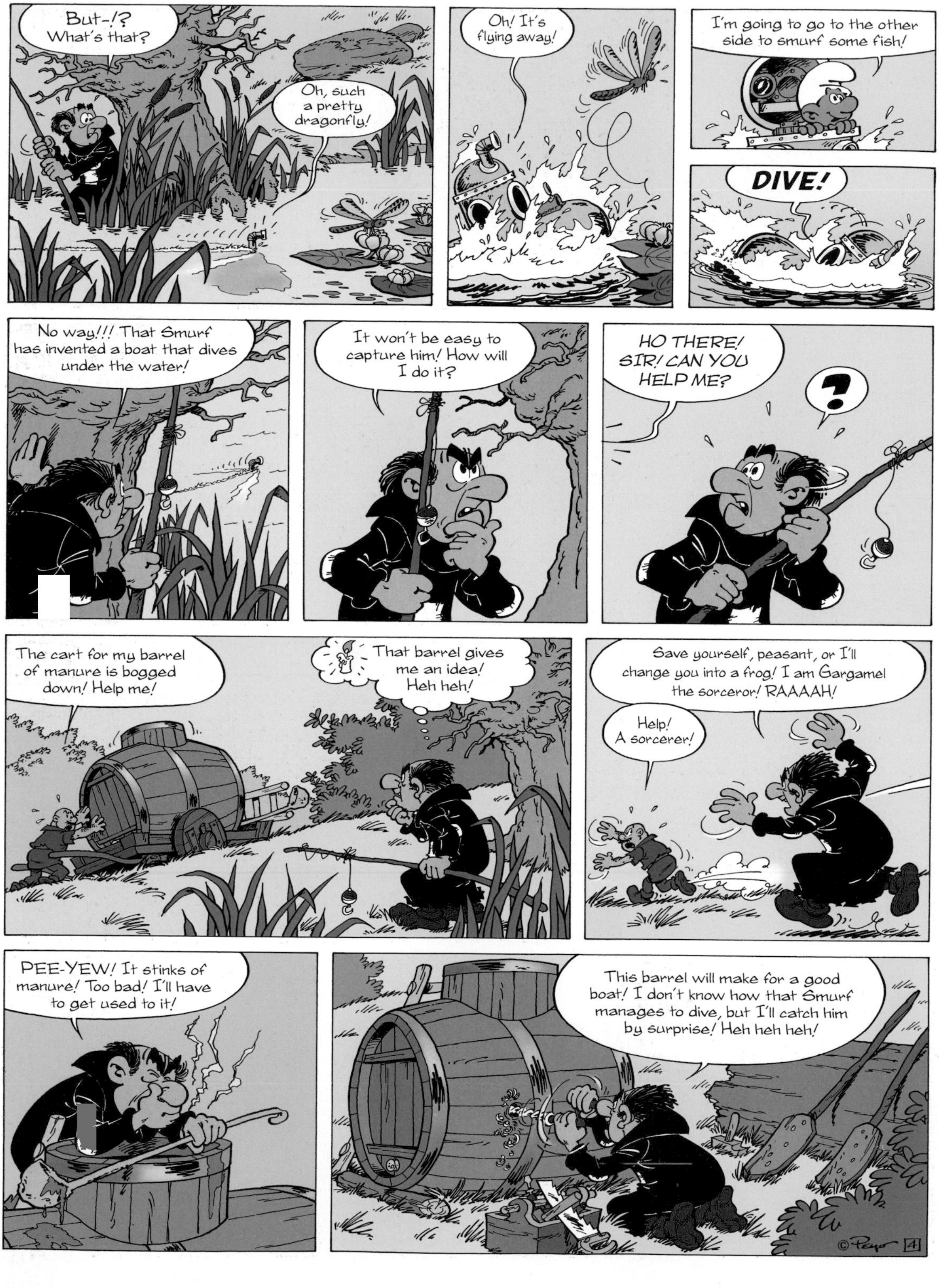
But-!? What's that?
Oh, such a pretty dragonfly!
Oh! It's flying away!
I'm going to go to the other side to smurf some fish!
DIVE!
No way!!! That Smurf has invented a boat that dives under the water!
It won't be easy to capture him! How will I do it?
HO THERE! SIR! CAN YOU HELP ME?
?
The cart for my barrel of manure is bogged down! Help me!
That barrel gives me an idea! Heh heh!
Save yourself, peasant, or I'll change you into a frog! I am Gargamel the sorceror! RAAAAH!
Help! A sorcerer!
PEE-YEW! It stinks of manure! Too bad! I'll have to get used to it!
This barrel will make for a good boat! I don't know how that Smurf manages to dive, but I'll catch him by surprise! Heh heh heh!
© Peyo
4

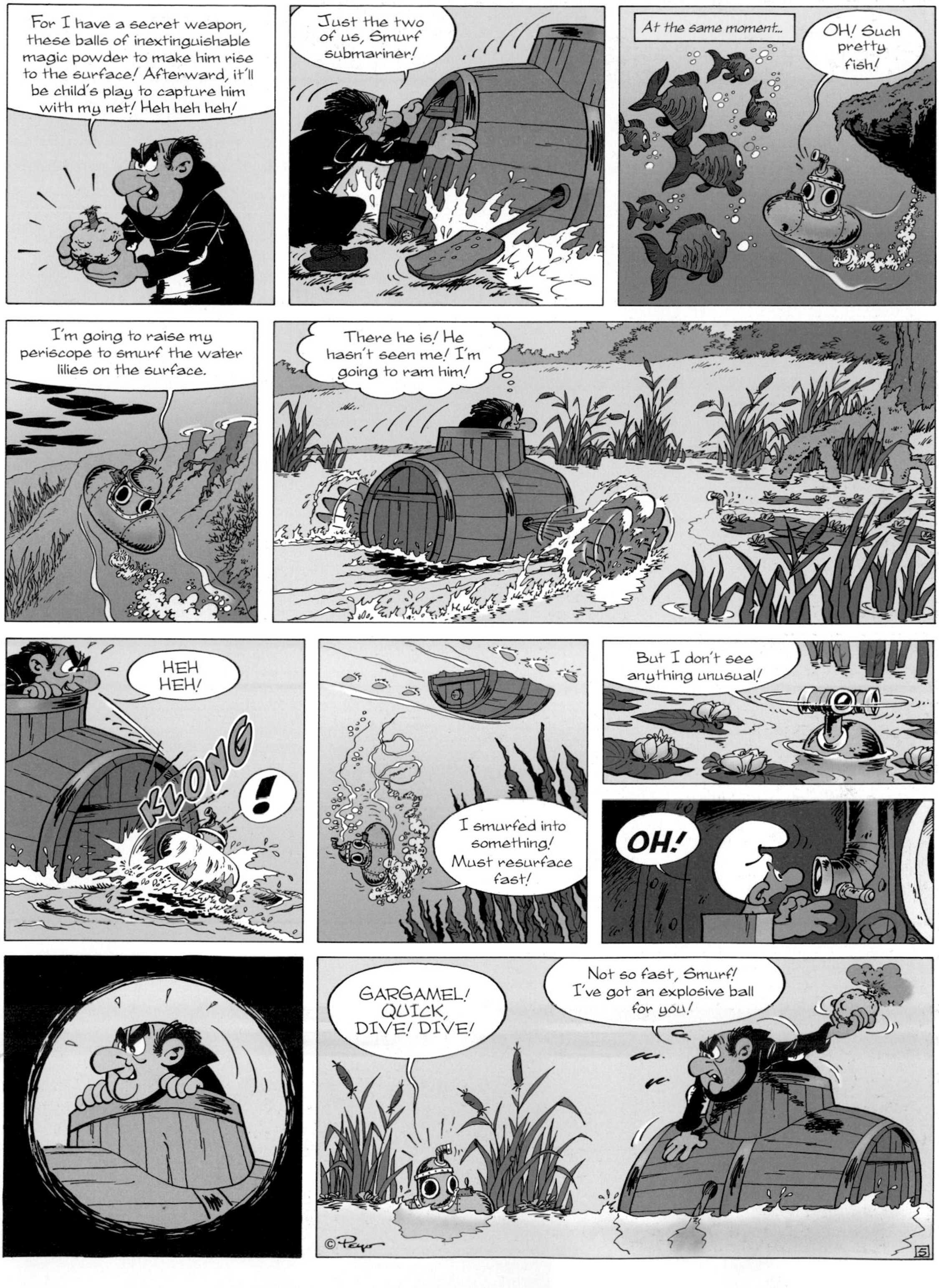
For I have a secret weapon, these balls of inextinguishable magic powder to make him rise to the surface! Afterward, it'll be child's play to capture him with my net! Heh heh heh!
Just the two of us, Smurf submariner!
At the same moment...
OH! Such pretty fish!
I'm going to raise my periscope to smurf the water lilies on the surface.
There he is! He hasn't seen me! I'm going to ram him!
HEH HEH!
KLONG
!
I smurfed into something! Must resurface fast!
But I don't see anything unusual!
OH!
GARGAMEL! QUICK, DIVE! DIVE!
Not so fast, Smurf! I've got an explosive ball for you!
© Peyo
5

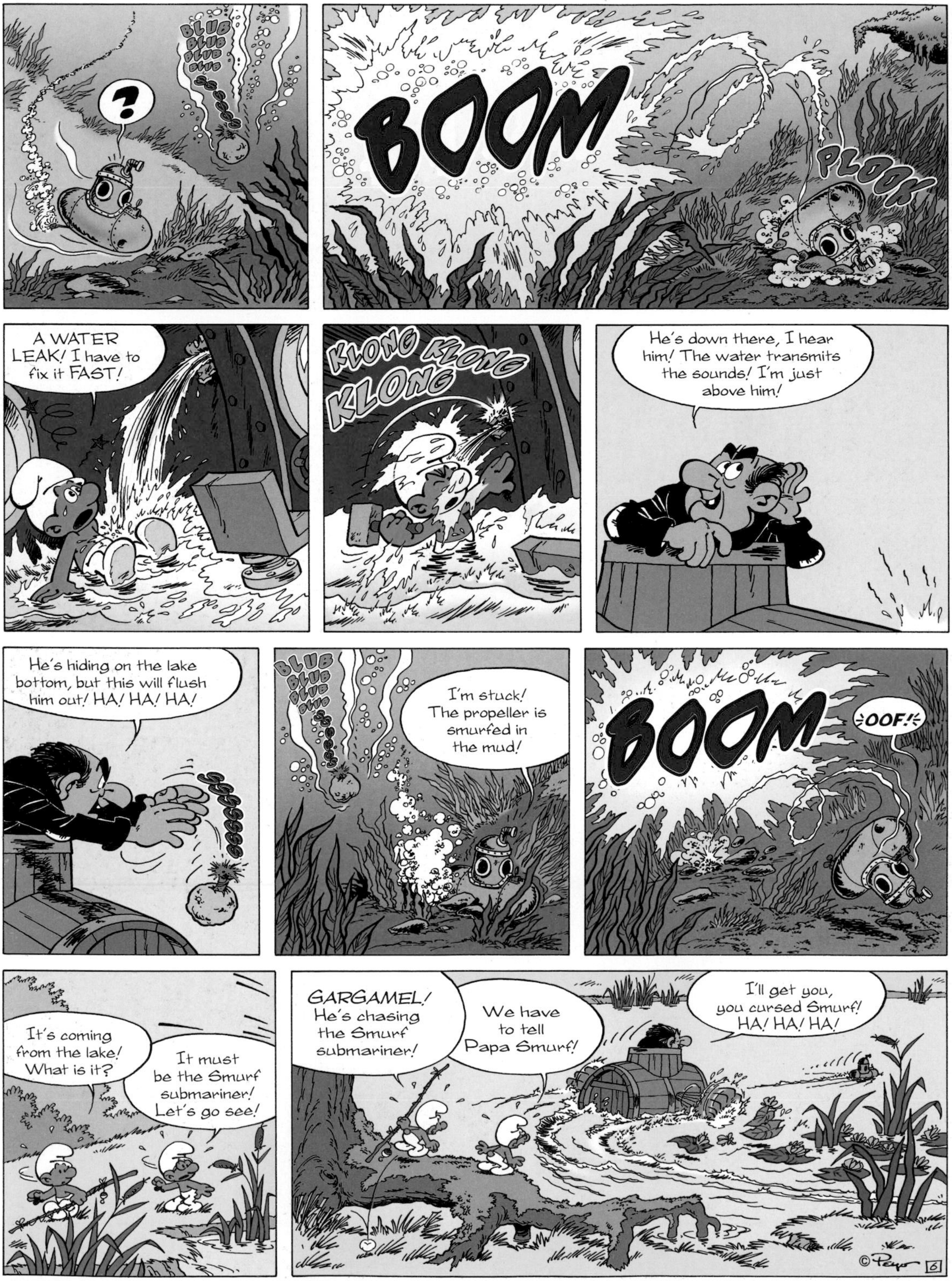
BLUB BLUB BLUB BLUB
SSSSSS
?
BOOM
PLOOK
A WATER LEAK! I have to fix it FAST!
KLONG KLONG KLONG
He's down there, I hear him! The water transmits the sounds! I'm just above him!
He's hiding on the lake bottom, but this will flush him out! HA! HA! HA!
SSSSSS
BLUB BLUB BLUB BLUB
SSSSSS
I'm stuck! The propeller is smurfed in the mud!
BOOM
OOF!
It's coming from the lake! What is it?
It must be the Smurf submariner! Let's go see!
GARGAMEL! He's chasing the Smurf submariner!
We have to tell Papa Smurf!
I'll get you, you cursed Smurf! HA! HA! HA!
© Peyo 6

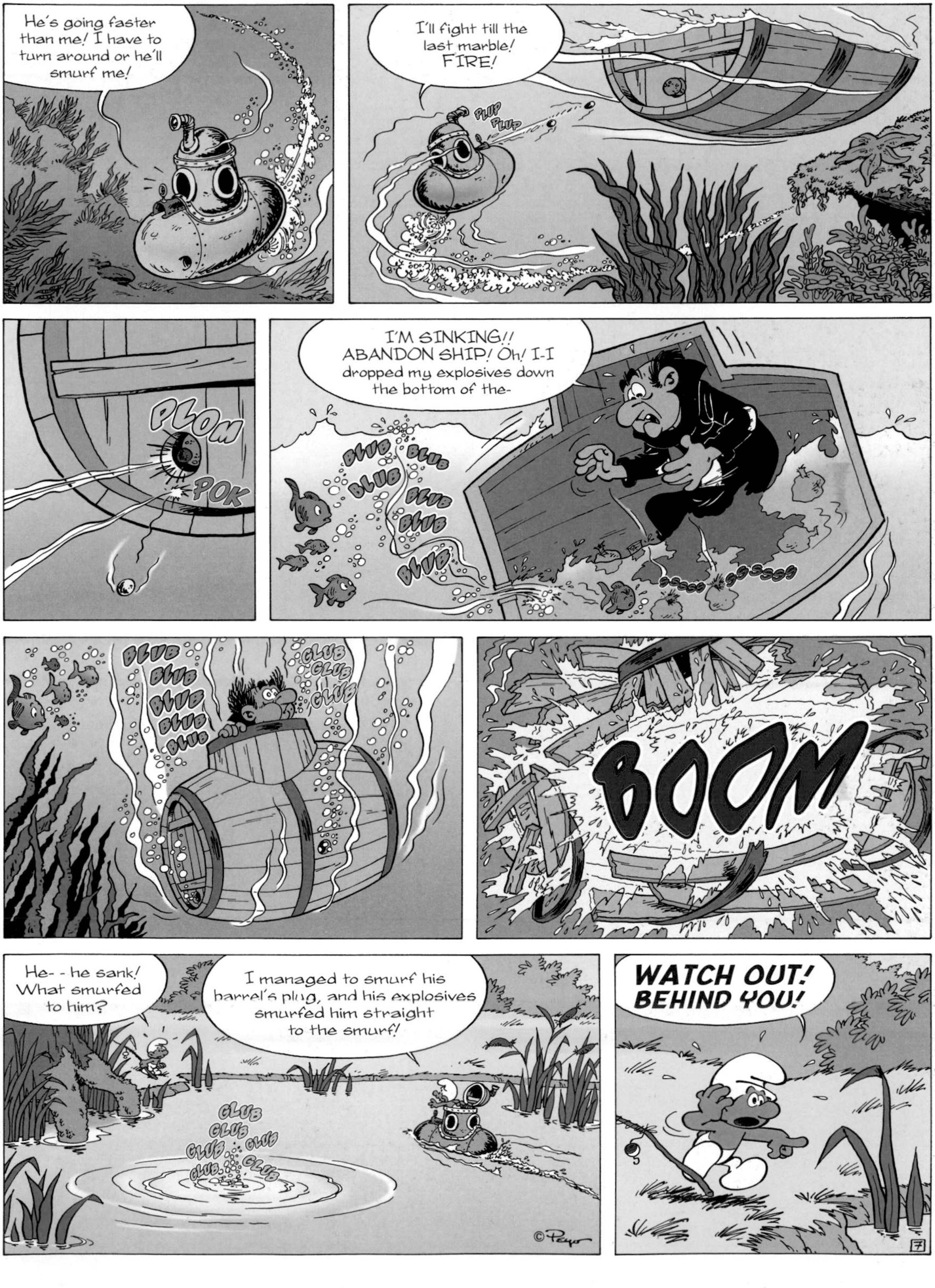
He's going faster than me! I have to turn around or he'll smurf me!
I'll fight till the last marble! FIRE!
PLUP PLUP
PLOM
POK
I'M SINKING!! ABANDON SHIP! Oh! I-I dropped my explosives down the bottom of the-
BLUB BLUB BLUB BLUB BLUB BLUB
BLUB BLUB BLUB BLUB BLUB
GLUB GLUB GLUB
BOOM
He- - he sank! What smurfed to him?
I managed to smurf his barrel's plug, and his explosives smurfed him straight to the smurf!
GLUB GLUB GLUB GLUB GLUB GLUB
WATCH OUT! BEHIND YOU!
© Peyo
7

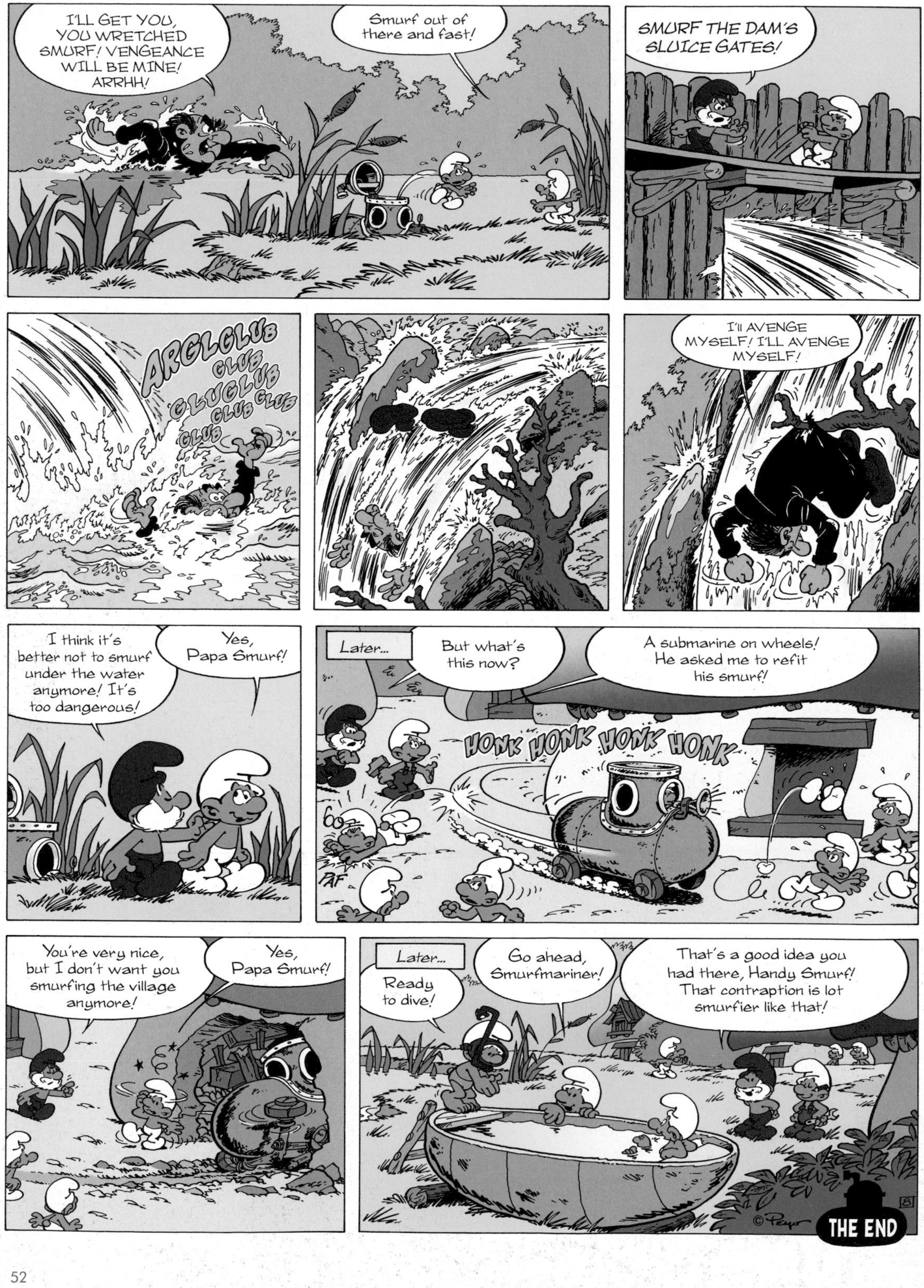
I'LL GET YOU, YOU WRETCHED SMURF! VENGEANCE WILL BE MINE! ARRHH!
Smurf out of there and fast!
SMURF THE DAM'S SLUICE GATES!
ARGLGLUB GLUB GLUGLUB GLUB GLUB GLUB
I'll AVENGE MYSELF! I'LL AVENGE MYSELF!
I think it's better not to smurf under the water anymore! It's too dangerous!
Yes, Papa Smurf!
Later...
But what's this now?
A submarine on wheels! He asked me to refit his smurf!
HONK HONK HONK HONK
PAF
You're very nice, but I don't want you smurfing the village anymore!
Yes, Papa Smurf!
Later...
Ready to dive!
Go ahead, Smurfmariner!
That's a good idea you had there, Handy Smurf! That contraption is lot smurfier like that!
© Peyo
THE END

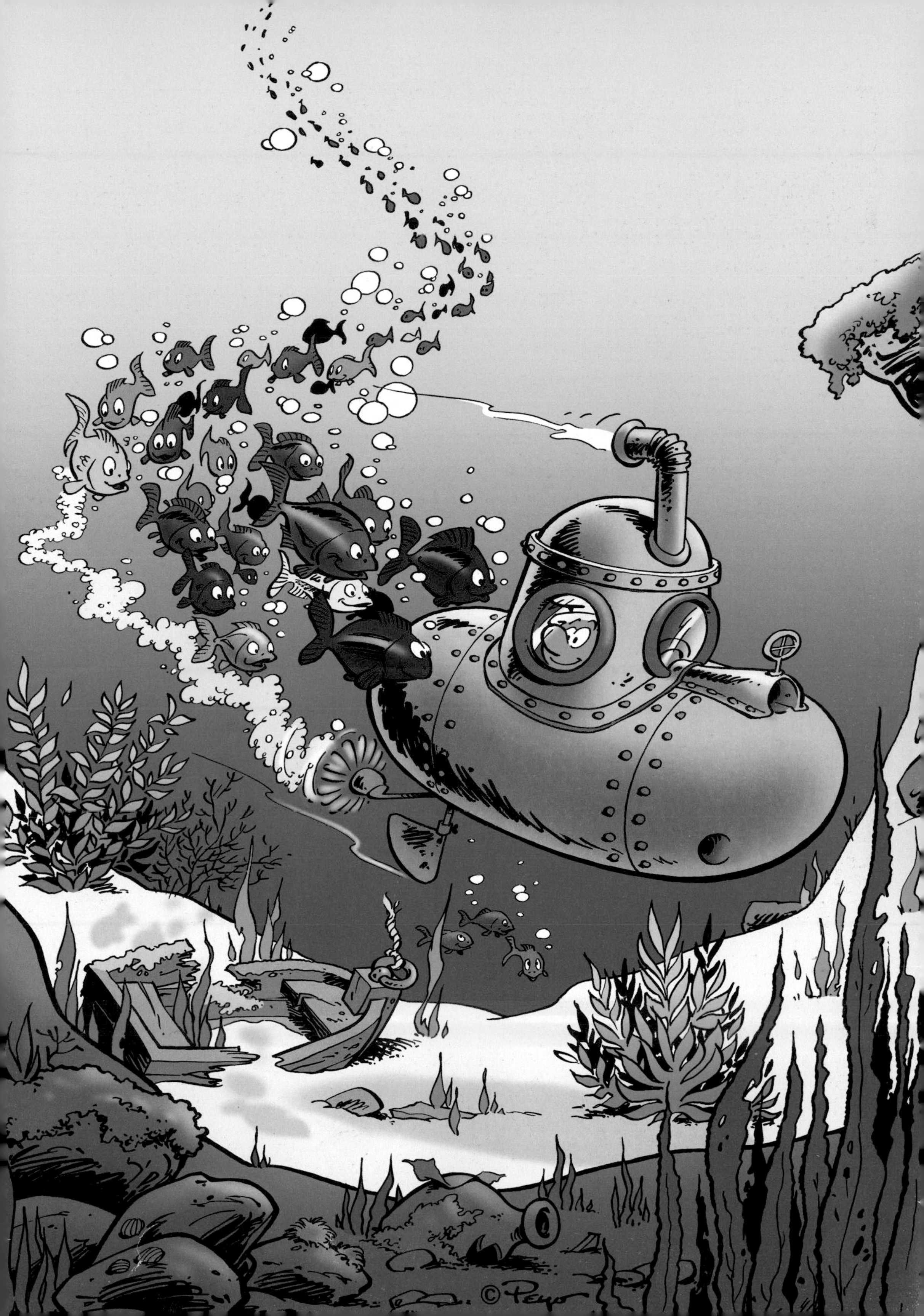
© Peyo

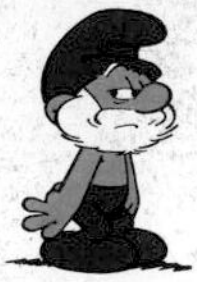

THE SMURFS COMIC STRIPS

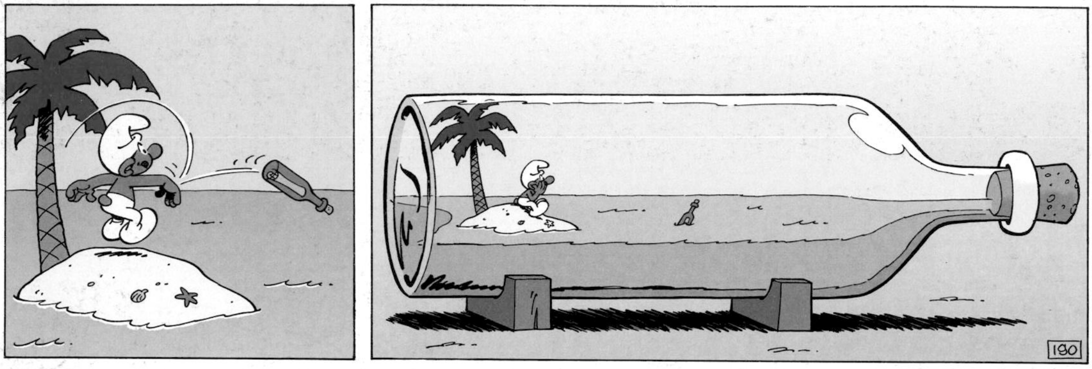

160

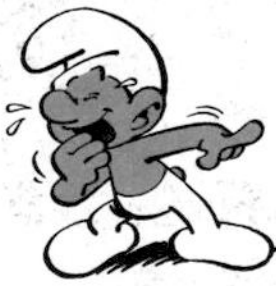

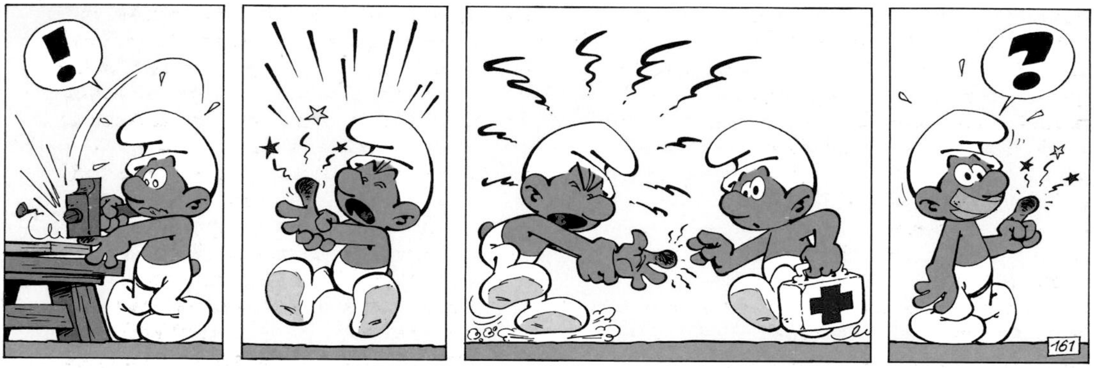

161

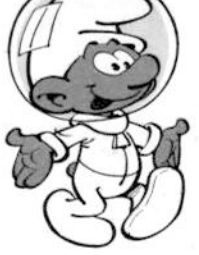

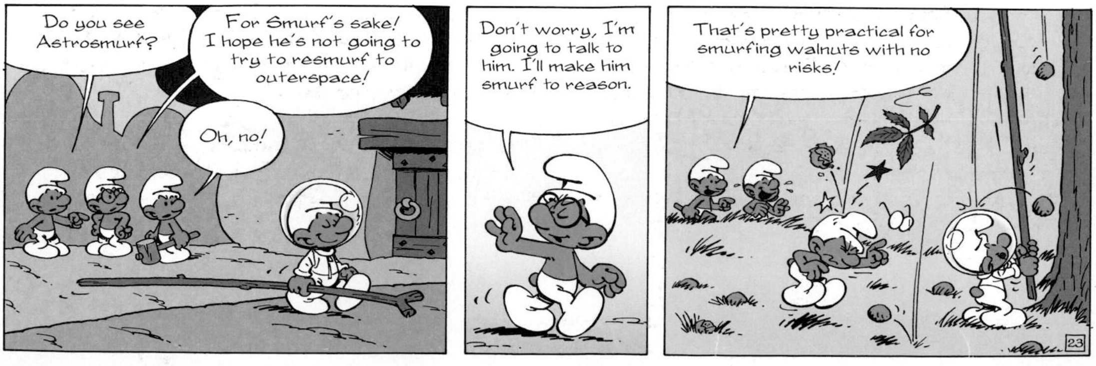

Do you see Astrosmurf?
For Smurf's sake! I hope he's not going to try to resmurf to outerspace!
Oh, no!
Don't worry, I'm going to talk to him. I'll make him smurf to reason.
That's pretty practical for smurfing walnuts with no risks!
23

WATCH OUT FOR PAPERCUTZ™

Welcome to the star-spanning, under-sea-faring, seventh SMURFS graphic novel from Papercutz, the scrappy, yet earthbound publisher of great graphic novels for all ages. I'm Jim Salicrup, your somewhat soggy Smurf-in-Chief, who is looking more and more like Gargamel as time goes on! Or, in other words, we're the folks who proudly publish Peyo's comic art masterpiece—THE SMURFS—in all-new editions.

If you're the curious type and you're wondering "who is this mysterious person known as Peyo?," then may I suggest you pick up Matt. Murray's new book, "The World of Smurfs," a celebration of tiny blue proportions? Not only is Mr. Murray our Smurfs Consultant, he's also America's leading Smurfologist—his blog (http://smurfology.blogspot.com/) is a great source of Smurfs-related news and trivia. But if you really want an informative overview of the entire history of the Smurfs—from the original comics by Peyo to the new 3D motion picture—then "The World of Smurfs" is the book for you!

Speaking of history, for all THE SMURFS comicbook completists, we should mention the special edition comicbooks that we published to help generate excitement for THE SMURFS graphic novel series. First, we published, a special preview comic for just one dollar—THE SMURFS Vol. 2, No. 1[1] in May 2010. Featuring an all-new cover, the special comicbook featured the very first appearances of Gargamel and Azrael in "The Smurfnapper," by Y. Delporte and Peyo. (Don't worry if you missed the comicbook, we'll be publishing "The Smurfnapper" in the Smurfs graphic novel #9 "Gargamel and the Smurfs!") Reaction at comicbook stores across America to the specially priced comicbook was predictably super-positive! Diamond Comics Distributors made the comic a special "Featured Item of the Month," which helped get comic shops excited about it. THE SMURFS were back, and fans wanted more, more, MORE!

Working with Sarah Martinez and our friends at Diamond Comic Distributors, we also produced

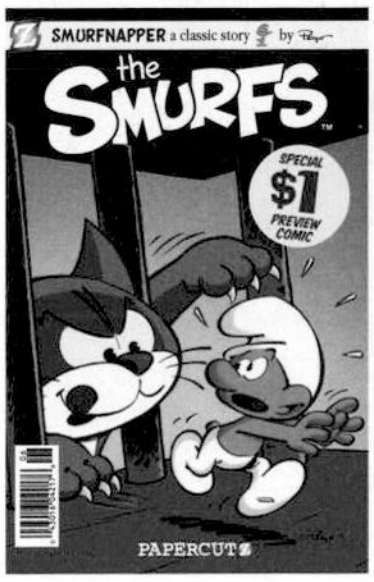
SMURFNAPPER a classic story by Peyo
the SMURFS
SPECIAL $1 PREVIEW COMIC
PAPERCUTZ

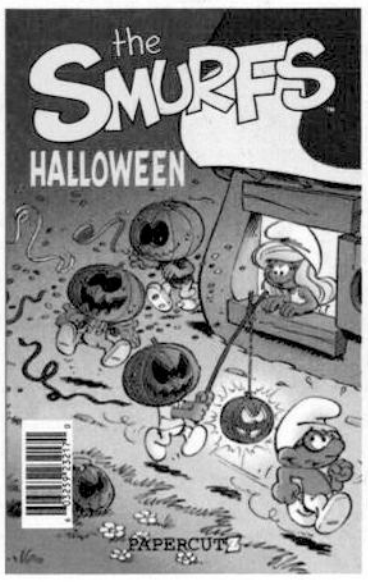
the SMURFS
HALLOWEEN
PAPERCUTZ

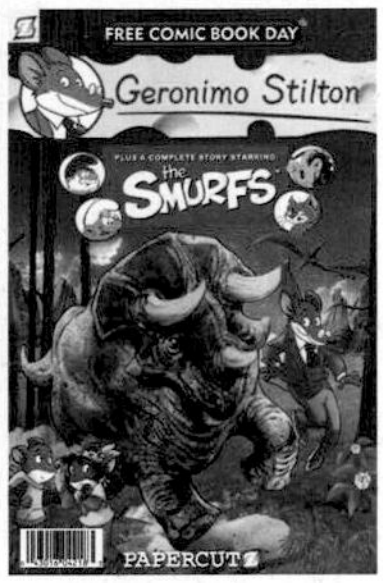
FREE COMIC BOOK DAY
Geronimo Stilton
the SMURFS
PAPERCUTZ

a very special SMURFS comicbook for Halloween 2010. Cleverly titled THE SMURFS HALLOWEEN, this mini-comic featured two Smurfs stories "Halloween" and "The Smurfs and the Little Ghost." These comics were designed to be given away at Halloween as special treats, and most comicbook stores gave them away for free.

Speaking of free, Papercutz was invited to participate in this year's Free Comic Book Day, which took place May 7th. We decided to go all out and create a special comic featuring a preview of our incredibly popular GERONIMO STILTON graphic novels, and as an extra-special bonus, we also included "The Smurf Submarine," which as sharp eyed Smurf fans already noticed, is also featured in this very graphic novel. Plus we threw in a sampling of the rarely-seen-in-America Smurfs comic strips (see page 54 for a few examples).

If you're really lucky, and you really, really want to include these comics in your collection, you can check with your favorite comicbook store to see if they still have any copies available, or if they can order some for you. To find the comicbook shop nearest you, call toll free 888 COMIC BOOK. But don't smurf it if you can't find 'em! All the Smurf stories in the comicbooks will be collected in the graphic novels sooner or later.

That's about all the Smurfiness we have room for this time around. Don't miss THE SMURFS graphic novel #8 "The Smurf Apprentice," coming soon! Stay Smurfy!

Smurfily yours,

Jim

[1] If you're a true SMURFS comicbook completist, we don't have to tell you that Marvel Comics published SMURFS Vol. 1, Nos. 1-3. As well as a SMURFS TREASURY EDITION, and a set of all new SMURFS mini-comics, back in 1983.